RYDER REVISITED

PAMELA M. KELLEY

PIPING PLOVER PRESS

PROLOGUE

"We need to do something about Ryder. It's time he found someone and got married," Gertrude Quinn said as she set a platter of raspberry jam filled thumbprint cookies in the center of the table. It was Wednesday afternoon and as usual, her friends Maude, Nellie, Betty and Ruby were over for tea. They'd met every Wednesday at Gertrude's home, Quinn Valley Ranch for ages. Ryder was one of Gertrude's many grandchildren and the oldest of five children born to her son Richard and his wife, Marcia, who was a widow.

"Has he been dating anyone?" Nellie asked as she reached for a cookie.

"Not as far as I know. Not seriously anyway. Not since that girl he dated in high school, Bethany. She was a lovely girl."

"She moved away, didn't she?" Betty asked.

"Yes, she went off to cooking school somewhere in

New England. I hear she's a chef somewhere in New York City now," Gertrude said.

"Speaking of chefs, has Ryder hired a new one yet?" Ruby asked.

"No, and I think he's been under a lot of stress after what happened." Gertrude made a face as if she'd tasted something unpleasant.

"Yes, that really was shocking," Maude said.

They all nodded in agreement as it had been quite a scandal.

"Marcia's been doing the cooking again, right?" Ruby asked.

"Yes, but that's just temporary, until they find a new chef," Gertrude said.

"You know, it's funny you mention Bethany. I could have sworn I saw her a few days ago at the grocery store," Betty said.

"She may be home visiting her mother as I know she's been sick. I don't expect that she'll stay long, unfortunately," Ruby said.

Gertrude was silent for a moment and looked deep in thought. "I'll talk to Marcia. She's friends with Bethany's mother. She can find out for us. It's a long shot, but you never know. Maybe we'll get lucky and Bethany will decide to stay a while...."

CHAPTER 1

Y ou look tired. Is the new computer system still driving you crazy?" Ryder Quinn leaned back in his seat at the bar of Quinn's Pub. He was worried that his mother was working too hard. He and his sister Maggie had bought her out last year, and she was supposed to be retired. But, given their recent drama, he was grateful for her help. It was Friday night, almost midnight, and the restaurant was empty except for the three of them.

His mother sat up straight and gave him 'the look'.

"Ryder Quinn. You should never tell a woman she looks tired. Ever. I'm fine. And I am getting used to that silly computer of yours. Maggie, honey, I'll take a splash of that new chardonnay." Even though the pub was closed, Maggie was still behind the bar, wiping the counter down.

Maggie laughed. "Mom's right, Ryder. Don't ever say that." He watched as she poured two glasses of wine, put one in front of their mother and brought her own to the other side of the bar. She settled into a chair between them and smiled at her mother.

"I heard a lot of compliments on Mom's food tonight. The regulars don't want her to ever leave." His mother looked pleased to hear it.

But Ryder still felt guilty that he was going to be away for the whole weekend. "It's not fair for her to be in the kitchen all day every day though. I can cancel my trip. I'm sure Brad will understand."

"Don't be ridiculous. Your college roommate is getting married, and you haven't had a day off in weeks. I can cook in my sleep. You know that," his mother assured him.

He also knew by the tone of her voice that the discussion was over.

"No one misses Gary's cooking. He'd really been letting things slide," Maggie added. It was true. Gary did a fine job at first, but over the past six months, it seemed as though he wasn't trying as hard. His specials were lackluster and even standard items didn't seem as good as they used to be.

"Gary and Suzanne have to turn up, eventually. Have you heard any updates from the police?" his mother asked.

"Nothing yet."

Maggie sighed. "I still can't believe they were stealing from us and for so long. I considered Suzanne a friend."

The betrayal stung for all of them. "Gary and I

used to have beers together after work. I never suspected it," he admitted.

"No wonder they were so insistent that we didn't need to computerize," his mother added dryly.

"I still can't believe we missed it." Ryder lifted his glass and took a sip. The beer was a new one, a local IPA and was his current favorite.

"Suzanne used to always brag that she made more tips than anyone else," Maggie said. "I never thought much of it, but it makes sense now."

His mother chuckled. "And she always made those elaborate birthday cakes for everyone. Probably so no one would suspect she was up to anything."

Ryder sighed. "They were clever about it too, not taking enough that it would be noticed."

He'd only discovered their scheme by accident when he picked up a handwritten order off the kitchen floor. It was lucky for him that it had missed the trash can. It was a week after the new computer system had gone in and there shouldn't have been any more hand-written orders for the kitchen. He'd matched up credit card receipts at the end of the night for the order amount and there wasn't one, which meant the customers had paid in cash. But, the amount of the order wasn't in the register. It was as if it had never happened.

That's when he realized that Suzanne had pock-eted the cash and that Gary was in on it too as he threw the order slip away as if it had never existed. Ryder took a long hard look at his orders and profits for the past few months and realized the deception had been going on for a long time.

He'd questioned them and both vehemently denied any wrongdoing. But the next day, neither showed up to work, and no one had heard from them since. That was two weeks ago and while Suzanne was easily replaced, it was taking longer than he'd expected to find a new chef.

"Any promising resumes come in?" he asked hopefully. He'd called all the local schools and posted an ad for a chef and put it in the Quinn Valley newspaper and online as well. His mother had insisted on handling the hiring since she was the one that had designed their menu and was the only true cook in the family. Ryder managed the day to day running of the restaurant and Maggie handled everything related to the bar.

His mother nodded and for a moment he thought he saw a flash of a smile, but it was gone just as fast. "They have been trickling in. I have a few interviews scheduled for tomorrow morning. I'll keep you posted."

"Oh, that's great news." The job market was tight and there weren't many qualified people to choose from in Quinn Valley. It was a small town, like the neighboring one, Riston, and while there were a lot of tourists that came to stay at the inn and enjoy the hot springs, there weren't a lot of year round residents. He'd also posted ads in the Riston and Lewiston papers, hoping to cast a wider net of applicants.

"Have you closed out the month yet?" Maggie

asked with a worried look. He nodded. He knew what she was really asking was if things were looking up. Unfortunately they were not.

"It was pretty dismal. Down another ten percent from the month before. I won't be taking a check again this week."

"Well, if you're not taking one, I won't either," Maggie said.

"I'm happy to help you out, if you need a short-term loan," his mother offered.

"No!" Both he and Maggie said at the same time and then laughed. "Thank you, but we want to do this ourselves. I know we can turn things around," Ryder said. It was important to him and to Maggie that they were able to run the business on their own.

His mother reached over and gave his hand a squeeze. "I know you can. I have complete faith in both of you. This is just a blip, a minor hiccup to get past."

That was one of the things he'd always loved about his mother. Marcia Quinn was one of the most positive people he knew. And she'd helped to install that belief in all five of her children—that with hard work and the will to succeed, they could do anything.

He looked around Quinn's Pub, at the gleaming dark wood bar and beams, the soft leather chairs and cheerful watercolor paintings on the walls, and the big windows that let in plenty of daylight and even now, a bit of moonlight. Quinn's Pub was a family restaurant with a bar area that closed at eleven sharp every night. On the weekends, they had local live music and during the week, they ran specials and fun events like music bingo to bring people in.

When his mother ran the restaurant and was in the kitchen, they had a reputation for excellent comfort food and a strong base of regular customers. But since she'd retired and Gary took over the kitchen, business had slowed. It wasn't an immediate slow down, but rather a decline that almost wasn't noticeable at first. And it wasn't helped any by Gary and Suzanne skimming some of the profits.

Some of the customers were starting to come back though, now that word was getting around that Marcia Quinn was in the kitchen again. But Ryder knew that he needed to get someone good in there as soon as possible so they could start rebuilding and so his mother could enjoy her retirement. He smiled thinking about what being retired meant to her.

She still came by the restaurant every day, often bringing a batch of homemade ravioli that they could run as a special or a batch of her blueberry muffins that they ate together for breakfast before the day got underway. He knew that she still liked to keep her pulse on the business and to visit with her children.

"Ryder, I have one request I'd like you to agree on before you head out for the weekend?" His mother took a sip of chardonnay and smiled, waiting for him to respond.

"What's that?" He was ready to agree to anything.

"If I meet someone and want to hire them, I want your permission to do so."

"I don't get to meet them first?" As the general manager, he felt like he should be involved.

"If we have to wait around for you, we could lose a good candidate. Besides, I believe the last hire was yours?" Ouch! She had him there. Gary had been his pick.

He sighed. "Of course. I trust you. If you meet someone that knocks your socks off, by all means hire them."

"Thanks, honey. I've always been good at reading people. I'll find us someone."

Ryder relaxed and began to look forward to his weekend away. The restaurant would be in good hands, and maybe his mother would surprise him and find someone that could start right away. Anyone would be better than Gary.

CHAPTER 2

Bethany Davis peered in her rearview mirror, smoothed a few strands of flyaway blonde hair into place and added a swipe of sandy pink lipstick. The time on her cell phone showed that she was still five minutes early for her interview. She glanced at the blue front door of Quinn's Pub and felt butterflies in her stomach. She'd been back in Quinn Valley for almost two weeks and she needed a job, fast. The chef position at Quinn's was the only local opening she'd seen advertised, and she really didn't want to have to commute to Lewiston which was over an hour away.

The original plan had been to come home, spend a week with her mother and then head back to Manhattan. But, her mother had downplayed how serious her condition was. She needed her and truth be told, Bethany wanted to stay. She'd always planned to return to Quinn Valley someday. And now that she didn't have a job to return to in New York, she didn't need to rush back anytime soon. But her savings was dwindling, and she needed to get something, anything soon.

But, could she work at Quinn's Pub? Would they even want her? To say she had mixed feelings was an understatement. But, beggars couldn't be choosers. She took a deep breath, grabbed her purse and got out of the car.

Barely a minute after she knocked on the front door, it opened and Bethany felt as though she'd fallen back in time. Ryder's mother, Marcia Quinn, stood there, just a hair over five feet tall, with her chin length shiny brown bob, her warm blue eyes and the smile that made everyone feel right at home.

She looked exactly the same as Bethany remembered, except maybe there were a few tiny lines here and there and a slightly thicker middle, but she looked wonderful. And she immediately pulled Bethany into a bear hug.

"You look just as lovely as I remember! Come in, let's have a cup of tea and catch up, shall we? You're still a tea drinker?"

Bethany nodded and followed Marcia into the well-equipped kitchen that was a sea of spotless stainless steel. Marcia stopped at a coffee station and poured hot water for both of them and added tea bags.

"Milk, sugar or honey?" she asked as she slid the cup towards Bethany.

"Nothing, thanks."

Marcia added a splash of milk and a heaping spoonful of sugar to her cup and gave it a stir.

"Let's go get comfortable, shall we?" She led the way into the dining room and to a booth with soft padded seats. Once they were both settled and sipping their tea, Marcia began the interview.

"It's been a long time since you've been gone from Quinn Valley. How long are you planning to stick around?"

Bethany smiled. Marcia never was one to beat around the bush. And she could understand her concern. She didn't want to be replacing the position again in a few months.

"My intention is to stay in Quinn Valley."

Marcia looked pleased to hear it. But also a bit confused. "Your resume is impressive. You've worked at some fine restaurants in Manhattan. Why would you leave that?"

Bethany took a deep breath. She knew some would think her decision was crazy. She was at the prime of her career now and it wouldn't be difficult to find a new position in NYC. She'd had several offers already as soon as word got out that she'd left her last role.

"I never intended to stay long-term in Manhattan," she began softly. "I love Quinn Valley and it was always my intention to come back here when the time was right."

"And the time is right now?" Marcia leaned forward in her chair, listening intently.

"It's as right as it's ever going to be. I was going to

stay in Manhattan another year or two," Bethany admitted. "I still have things to learn and when I came home, it was just going to be for a visit. But, I've changed my mind and have decided it's time to stay."

There was a long moment of silence as Bethany debated how much to share. But then Marcia asked, "How is your mother doing?" Her tone was so kind and caring that Bethany was surprised to feel her eyes watering as the emotion welled up.

It had been a stressful two weeks since she'd been home. Her mother was her rock, and it had been a shock to see her so weak and sick. She wasn't sure, by the way Marcia said it, if she knew what was going on with her mother.

"She hasn't been well. But she's on the mend. I'm not sure if you've heard, but she has breast cancer."

"I did hear, and I'm very sorry." Bethany wasn't sure, but for a moment, Marcia's eyes looked a bit damp.

"Thank you. It's very treatable, stage one and has an excellent prognosis," she assured her. "She didn't tell me right away because she didn't want me to worry. She's had radiation and just finished with chemotherapy. It seems to be working well, but she's been very tired and not up to doing much."

"I can imagine. Please give her a hug from me. I told her I'd stop by whenever she's up for company. We're actually in a book club together and I see her often."

Bethany smiled. "I'll do that." She looked around

the room at the warm dark wood, polished brass trim and the light that poured through the large bay windows. It was a cozy place, and cheerful. She could imagine herself working there.

"I own a condo in Manhattan but will eventually put it on the market and buy something here in Quinn Valley. For now I'm staying with my mother."

"I'm sure she is thrilled to have your company." Marcia picked up Bethany's resume, and they talked for a bit about the different restaurants she'd worked at and what the focus of each had been.

"I've heard of some of these places. Are you sure Quinn's Pub will be enough for you? We're not terribly fancy here." For the first time, Marcia looked worried.

"I'm not interested in fancy. I like to make good food. Meals that people crave. Comfort food."

Marcia looked delighted to hear that. "Really? What's your favorite comfort food meal?"

Bethany laughed. "That's easy. I make an insanely good turkey pot pie. Or rotisserie chicken. It's all good. My short ribs and mashed potatoes are pretty amazing too."

"Those are both favorites of mine," Marcia said.

"The short-ribs takes hours to braise, but if you have a leftover chicken or turkey on hand, I could whip up a pot pie pretty quickly," Bethany offered. "We could keep chatting while I do it."

"That's a fabulous idea. I usually ask candidates to make a dish, but given where you've worked, I know you can do the job. If you don't mind though, it would be lovely to see how you work and taste your pot pie."

"I'm happy to do it and I'd love to get the feel of your kitchen. It looks like it has just about everything I'd need."

Marcia beamed. "It does. I designed it myself. And we have a few roasted chickens in the refrigerator. I was going to make chicken salad, but we can use one for a pot pie."

When they stood to head into the kitchen, Marcia froze for a moment as she faced the big bay window that looked out over the sidewalk. She looked like she'd seen a ghost or was maybe about to faint.

"Is everything okay?" Bethany asked.

Marcia turned her way and smiled though she still seemed a bit shaken. "Oh, everything's fantastic. I just thought I saw someone I knew for a minute there. An old friend that I haven't seen in years. But I'm sure it was someone else. Follow me."

Marcia showed her where everything was in the kitchen and they continued chatting while Bethany worked. She quickly made a pie crust first and Marcia looked surprised when she asked for vodka.

"That's a first," Marcia said as she handed her a bottle of vodka.

Bethany added a generous splash of it to the dough. "I learned this trick a few years ago. A little vodka makes for a light and flaky crust."

"Well, isn't that something?"

Once the crust was done, Bethany moved on to a saute pan where she added a generous glob of butter and some sliced onions. Once they were browned, she added chicken broth and sliced cooked carrots and potatoes and shredded chicken that she'd tossed with a bit of flour, salt and pepper. She stirred it all together and a few minutes after the mixture thickened up, she poured it into a pie pan lined with the dough. She added the top crust, poked a few holes in it for ventilation and slid it into the heated oven.

While the pie cooked, she and Marcia continued talking, moving past her experience and onto people they knew in common in Quinn Valley. Marcia caught her up on just about everyone.

"Oh, and there's another amazing chef in town. Do you like tacos?"

Bethany laughed. "Of course. Who doesn't like tacos?"

"Right. Silly question. Anyway, you must stop by Ciran's Taco Truck. He spent time in Texas and studied taco making. He's also back with his high school sweetheart, Roxane."

"I remember Ciran. I thought he was going to be a lawyer? Or maybe I remembered that wrong?"

"No, he was. He did. But tacos are his true passion."

Bethany smiled. "Well, I'd much rather make tacos than be a lawyer too." She hesitated and then asked the question she'd been dying to ask since she walked through the door. "How's Ryder doing?" Marcia had mentioned everyone they had in common, except her oldest son.

A curious gleam came into Marcia's eyes. "I'm so glad you asked. Ryder is fantastic. Better than ever. He's away this weekend at his college roommate's wedding. Otherwise he'd be here."

"He still works in the pub?" Bethany had known it was possible, likely even, but she hadn't been sure. She'd known he'd gone to college and was going to study business. At one point, she'd known everything Ryder wanted to do, all his hopes and dreams. But those dreams had included her and when she broke his heart, he'd cut her out of his life.

"He and Maggie bought me out a little over a year ago. Maggie runs the bar and Ryder oversees all the overall operations." Bethany's heart sank. Ryder was in charge. And there was probably no way he'd approve hiring her.

"So, I'll have to meet with Ryder too?" She was already dreading it.

But Marcia cheerfully shook her head. "No, that won't be necessary."

"No?" Bethany wasn't sure if she'd heard right.

"Ryder gave me permission to hire whoever I like. I told him to trust me."

Bethany wondered if his mother knew what she was doing. She couldn't imagine that Ryder would be happy about this, if she was offered the job without his input.

"I can't wait to try your pie. It smells delicious." Marcia smiled as she changed the subject.

Bethany could tell by the smell that the pie was ready. Some chefs went by a timer and a recipe, but she went by feel and taste and smell. She pulled the pie out of the oven and it was perfectly golden brown. She found two small plates and a spatula and scooped some of the pie onto each plate. She looked around for forks and Marcia was holding two of them. She handed one to Bethany and took a bite.

Bethany watched and waited for Marcia's verdict. Marcia took another bite, closed her eyes and made a happy sound.

"Mmmmm. Bethany, I make a good pot pie myself, but this is outstanding. Really exceptional."

Bethany was pleased to hear it. Nothing made her happier than hearing that people enjoyed her food. "I'm so glad you like it."

"I was going to offer you the job anyway," Marcia admitted. "How soon do you think you could start?"

"As soon as you want me."

"If you like, you could start tonight and work side by side with me. I could use the help as Saturdays can be busy."

Bethany grinned. "I'd love to."

CHAPTER 3

Ryder was unusually relaxed and refreshed as he walked into the dining room of Quinn's Pub Monday morning. Taking the weekend off and spending time with his old friends was exactly what he'd needed. He'd liked Jenna, Brad's new wife, the moment he met her. She and Brad fit together so well—it was as if they'd been together for years. He'd been skeptical at first when Brad said he'd proposed to a girl he'd only been dating for a few months, but when he met her, he understood.

When Jenna and Brad weren't teasing each other, the love in their eyes was evident. Ryder was happy for his friend even if it made him a little sad for himself. He'd thought he'd found that kind of love once too, but it hadn't lasted. He put all his energy into the restaurant and while he dated often, no one had captured his heart since.

"What smells so good?" he asked as he slid into the

booth where his mother and sister sat drinking coffee and eating some kind of muffin. His mother put one on a plate and slid it over to him.

"Zen muffins, try a bite."

He broke off a piece and popped it in his mouth. A rush of cinnamon, nutmeg, ginger and something unusually fragrant... lavender, maybe? collided with shredded carrots and raisins. The muffin was hot from the oven and it was delicious. As he continued to eat, a curious calmness came over him. The muffins were aptly named. Or maybe he'd just had a good night's sleep for the first time in a long time.

"New recipe? You've outdone yourself this time. These are really good."

His mother smiled mischievously, and he wondered what she was up to.

"Not me. Our new chef."

He raised his eyebrows. "You hired someone? You didn't mention anything when I checked in last night."

"I didn't want you thinking about work while you were off having fun. Just remember, you gave me permission to hire anyone I wanted."

"Yes, we talked about that." What was she going on about?

"Well, I just wanted to remind you, that this can't be undone."

"Who did you hire?" His mother was acting so strange.

"Oh, here she comes now." Ryder heard footsteps

coming up behind him. "I think you remember Bethany Davis?"

"Hi Ryder. It's good to see you." Bethany's voice was soft and a little nervous. Ryder looked her way and felt a rush of emotions, everything from anger to confusion to attraction. Bethany looked even more beautiful than he remembered. Her hair was glossy and still so blonde. Lemon pie blonde he used to call it. It fell into long curls that she tied back in a ponytail. A few stray pieces fell in tendrils to frame her face.

And her eyes were as big and blue-gray as he remembered. She had a small straight nose and full lips. He used to love watching them as she tasted a ripe strawberry or as they came his way. He could kiss those sweet lips for hours and he had.

She was still as trim as he remembered, which was impressive considering that he knew she'd been working as a chef for years. Most chefs he'd met were not thin. Bethany was slim and small. She was just a few inches taller than his mother who didn't quite hit five feet, no matter how tall she stood.

Ryder looked at Bethany and then back at his mother. He didn't quite know what to say. His whole world had changed, just like that.

"How long are you in town for?" he finally managed.

"I'm here for good now." For good. Why now? Why his restaurant?

There was a long, awkward moment of silence as

both his sister and mother watched the two of them with fascination. It was too much for Ryder to take in.

"I'll be in my office." He stood and took the rest of his muffin with him. The last thing he saw as he walked away was the warmth and concern in Bethany's eyes. What was his mother thinking offering her a job? And what was she thinking by taking it?

BETHANY FELT LIKE ALL THE AIR HAD RUSHED OUT of the room when she laid eyes on Ryder that morning. She hadn't seen him in so long and he'd looked so good, with that thick, wavy hair that he always wore a little too long, the scruffy shadow along his jaw, that deep single dimple in his cheek when he smiled, and those eyes. Ryder's green eyes always seemed to look right through her. But this morning they'd held so much emotion. She could sense a mix of confusion, betrayal, anger, curiosity and attraction.

On some level it was reassuring to see that the attraction was still there. It had always been strong between them. It had been so hard to leave Ryder. And no matter how she'd tried to explain, she knew that he'd never understood why she had to go. She wondered if he could ever forgive her and she was curious if there was anyone in his life. She knew he wasn't married. She would have heard about that. Her best friend, Jill, still lived in Quinn Valley and she would have heard about that as it was a very small town. Too small it sometimes seemed as everyone knew everyone else's business.

She hoped that it wasn't going to be too awkward working together. They were not off to a promising start. But she knew that Ryder had been blind-sided. She hadn't realized until that morning that his mother hadn't filled him in about his new chef. Maybe Marcia thought it would be easier somehow, she wasn't sure about that.

Or maybe Ryder just needed time to digest it. He'd never been one for sudden changes. She was glad she'd made her zen muffins for them that morning. The ginger and lavender had calming properties, and she'd had a feeling Ryder could use a little zen that morning of all days.

At a little past three, she felt his energy around her and glanced up. Ryder stood in front of the line, looking deep in thought. She guessed that he was ready for something to eat.

"What can I get for you?" she asked.

He looked wary. "I don't know. What's already made? I don't want you to go to any trouble." Or maybe he was so hungry that he didn't want to wait anymore.

She smiled. "It's no trouble. I have a tray of braised short ribs that are ready. I could plate that right up with some mashed potatoes and sautéed spinach."

"Sure. That sounds good."

She piled a plate high with food and added a generous drizzle of gravy over the short ribs and potatoes.

"Here you go. Hope you like it."

"Thanks. It smells great." He took the plate and walked off. Once he was gone, the air in the room suddenly felt flat.....the charged energy had deflated.

A half hour later, Ryder brought his empty plate back to the kitchen and handed it to the dishwasher. He strolled back over to the line and looked at her curiously.

"Those were the best short ribs I've ever had, anywhere. And I've had my fair share." He seemed almost angry as he said the words.

"Thank you."

There was a long awkward moment of silence before he finally broke it by asking,"Why are you here? This restaurant, of all places?"

Bethany shrugged. "It was the only opening in the area. I didn't want to commute to Lewiston."

"I wouldn't want to do that either," he admitted. He turned to leave and then added, "I heard about your mother. I'm sorry. Please tell her I asked for her."

"I will."

He nodded and then left again and Bethany felt tears come to her eyes. It had been a long day and ever since she'd been home, she'd been feeling emotional. It was harder than she'd thought it would be to see Ryder again, and to be around him. Her mother had adored Ryder and at first hadn't understood why Bethany needed to go to New York when she could have just stayed in Quinn Valley and married him.

But at nineteen, she had wanted more. She needed

to experience life outside Quinn Valley and to become the chef she wanted to be, she'd needed to work at the best restaurants. She'd wondered more than once if she'd made a mistake, but in her heart, she knew that she'd done the right thing, the only thing, that she could, for herself.

WHEN BETHANY WALKED IN THE FRONT DOOR, HER mother was curled up on the living room sofa, with a soft fleece blanket wrapped around her. Her mother's oversized orange cat, Simon, was sprawled across the back of the sofa and didn't even glance Bethany's way as she entered the room.

"Hi, honey, how was your day?"

Bethany knew that her mother was secretly hoping that Bethany and Ryder might get back together now that they'd be working together. But Ryder had made it clear when she left for New York that it was over for them. He'd immediately started dating Natalie Palmer, who graduated high school with them and had been a cheerleader and active on the beauty pageant circuit. Although she also knew that hadn't lasted long. She hadn't been home often after that, just for an occasional long weekend when she could get away, so she hadn't run into him before now.

She sighed. If her mother had seen Ryder's lack of enthusiasm when he saw her, she wouldn't be as hopeful. Bethany just hoped they'd be able to work together. She flopped onto the love seat facing the other sofa.

"It was pretty good. I like it there for the most part." If Ryder wasn't there, it would be ideal. She loved the kitchen, and it was the perfect place for the type of food she wanted to focus on. Marcia welcomed her ideas for new menu items and specials and while he'd been less than happy to see her there, Ryder at least seemed to like her food.

"Did you see Ryder?"

"I did. You should have seen the look on his face when he realized that his mother had hired me while he was gone. If they weren't so desperate for a chef, I think he might have told her to keep looking."

"Oh, that's too bad. I thought he might be happy to see you." The light went out of her eyes a little and Bethany knew she was disappointed. She was too. Though she didn't share her mother's hope that they'd reunite, she was hoping that since so many years had passed that he'd be glad to see her at least as a friend.

"I'm sure it will be fine, once he has a chance to digest it all. Ryder never did like surprises." Her stomach rumbled, and she realized she hadn't eaten since lunch.

"I'm going to make a green drink, would you like one?"

"That sounds nice, honey. The one you made this morning was delicious."

Bethany went to the kitchen and returned a few minutes later with a cold juice smoothie for both of them. She'd juiced green apples, beets, ginger, carrots and kale. The combination of fruits and veggies had a sweet fresh taste, and it was a way to get healthy, organic nutrients into her mother.

She was trying to build up her immune system to support the chemotherapy and help her mother heal faster. She'd just had her last treatment a few days ago and her doctor said if all went well, she could be cancer free soon. Bethany handed her mother her drink and settled back on the sofa with her own.

"Thanks. Are you working next Tuesday night?" her mother asked.

"I'll be working on Tuesday but my regular hours are going to be ten to seven or so during the week and later on Saturday nights. I'll get all their daily specials prepped and get them through lunch and dinner and Bryan, the sous chef will finish up. Is something going on Tuesday?"

Her mother smiled. "The girls asked if I might be up for music bingo. I haven't been for weeks and I think I might be ready to get out again. You could join us if you're not working."

Bethany was thrilled that her mother was feeling up to going out soon.

"I'd love that. I can just join you all when I finish up."

"Good. We need someone young on our team. There's always music we have no idea about."

Bethany laughed. "I'll try my best. But I wouldn't get your hopes up."

CHAPTER 4

Ryder leaned against the bar waiting for Maggie to finish up a phone call so they could go over the bar order. While he waited, he glanced over at his grandmother, Gertrude Quinn, and her cronies, Betty, Maude, Nellie and Ruby as they enjoyed their late lunch. It was half-past three, and the restaurant was almost empty except for their round table by the window. He'd noticed Grandma glance his way more than once in the past ten minutes, and he was pretty sure that he wasn't imagining that she looked quite pleased with herself.

Maggie was also smiling as she hung up the phone and turned his way.

"Do you think it's possible to fall in love with someone's voice? I look forward to calling my order into Charlie Harris every week just to listen to him talk."

Ryder laughed. "Anything's possible. Have you ever met him?"

"No. And he probably looks nothing like I imagine. I picture a young Brad Pitt or Bradley Cooper. I don't even know if he's single. He's probably happily married with five kids."

Ryder thought for a moment. "It's been a long time since I've run into Charlie, but last I knew, I think he was single."

Maggie sighed. "I know I'm being silly. The last thing I'm looking for anyway is a new relationship."

"It has been a while, Mags. It might be time to get back out there," he said gently. Maggie had ended her last relationship almost a year ago and hadn't really dated anyone more than once or twice since.

"It's not time yet, Ryder. I'll know when it is." She said firmly as two new customers walked up to the bar.

Ryder noticed his grandmother and two of her friends looking his way again.

"What is Grandma up to? Do you have any idea?"

Maggie looked surprised. "I haven't the foggiest. Why don't you go ask her?"

"I think I will." He strolled over to the table of women and his grandmother beamed when she saw him coming their way.

"There's my favorite grandson! We were just talking about you." Ryder knew that she said that to all her grandsons, but it was still nice to hear.

"I thought my ears were ringing. All good things, I hope?" he teased.

"Of course. We were just saying how smart you

were to hire Bethany. She's a marvelous chef. I always did like her you know."

Ryder sighed. His grandmother loved to play matchmaker. But he needed to nip this in the bud fast. Once she had her mind set on something, she was known to be relentless.

"She is a very talented chef. I agree. But I'm sure this is a short-term thing for her and she'll be going back to Manhattan once her mother is better."

"Oh, I think you're wrong about that. We heard that she's here to stay."

"Why would she want to stay in Quinn Valley? She couldn't wait to leave years ago."

His grandmother gave his arm a squeeze and smiled as if she found him amusing and maybe a little dim. "Oh, I can think of lots of reasons why she might want to stick around. We'll just have to wait and see, I suppose. Please tell her how much we enjoyed everything today. I've never had such a delicious macaroni and cheese."

"I'll tell her. It was nice seeing you, Gram, ladies." He nodded at the rest of the women who all looked almost as excited about his love life as his grandmother did.

～

BETHANY DIDN'T SEE RYDER UNTIL LATER THAT afternoon, a little after four when she set out the evening staff meal and was writing up the evening specials.

"What are you serving us tonight?" he asked as he strolled into the kitchen. He almost sounded friendly, which was a nice surprise. She'd made one of her favorite meals for the staff and was pleased to see that so far it was a hit with just about everyone. They had the option to eat the provided meal before their shift or to order something off the menu and pay half price.

"It's a chicken stir-fry over wild mushroom risotto."

"Sounds good." He grabbed a plate and helped himself to a little of both. "My grandmother was in earlier. She said to tell you hello. She liked your mac and cheese. She insisted that I tell you that too." He smiled as he went to take a bite of risotto.

"Please tell her hello as well, next time you see her."

"I will." He stood quietly eating for a few minutes while she finished writing the specials on the whiteboard.

"Are you having any trouble with the computer system?" he asked. "We just started using it a few weeks ago."

"We actually used the same program at the last two places I worked. So that made it easy."

"Good. Our last chef wasn't a fan of it." He told her the story of how his chef and one of the waitresses had been pocketing money from customers that paid with cash.

"I'm sorry to hear that. Unfortunately, you're not

alone. Something like that has happened at a few different places I've worked at."

"Oddly enough, that does make me feel a little better. I was feeling pretty foolish that I didn't figure out what they were up to sooner," he admitted.

The kitchen door swung open and Ryder's brother, David, walked in.

"There you are! Maggie told me you were in your office." He glanced Bethany's way. "She also told me that you're the new chef here. It's great to see you again. It's been a while."

Bethany smiled. "It has. Good to see you too David." She knew that she'd be ordering most of her food supplies from David as he ran a local restaurant food distribution service. And Ryder's other brother, Carter, was one of his suppliers. He raised organic live-stock and produce.

"I was on my way back there. You hungry?"

David shook his head. "No, I had a big lunch. It smells good though."

"Alright, let's head to my office then."

"Bye, Bethany," David said as the two brothers walked off. She watched them go thinking how similar they looked. All the Quinn boys had that same, single dimple and were all tall with thick, dark hair. Yet their personalities were very different. David was friendly and outgoing while Ryder was more reserved and somewhat intense. She'd been so drawn to him in high school and even know, she had to admit, that for her, the attraction was still there.

~

A LITTLE PAST SEVEN, AFTER THE DINNER RUSH was winding down, Tom, her line cook and assistant, assured her he was fine handling things for the rest of the night. Bethany took off her apron and grabbed her purse. She'd planned to go straight home, but Jill had texted that some friends who recently got married were in town and they were going to have a few drinks at Quinn's and she should join them. She ducked into the ladies room, quickly ran a brush through her hair after taking it out of the elastic ponytail holder and added a little lipstick.

As soon as she walked into the dining room, she saw Jill sitting at a table with a couple. Jill waved as soon as she saw her and Bethany slid into the empty chair.

"Bethany, this is Cameron and Ethan. I work with Cameron, she's a nurse at the hospital. She and Ethan are on their honeymoon!" Jill's practice was located in Quinn Valley, but as an ob/gyn doctor she was often at the Riston hospital delivering babies.

"Congratulations!" The two of them looked very much in love as Cameron told her how they'd known each other since elementary school, but it was actually Ethan's grandmother who played matchmaker after having Cameron for a nurse.

"I agreed to marry Ethan because it was only going to be for a month."

"But then, I won her over with my irresistible charm," Ethan said with a grin.

"You did, actually!" She leaned over and gave him a sweet peck on his cheek.

"Are you staying at the inn?" Bethany asked. The Quinn family ran the nicest hotel in the area, close to the natural hot springs.

"We are. It's a lovely getaway. We are here for the rest of the week and it's nice to be so close to home."

"We'll do a longer vacation in the Caribbean later this year," Ethan added.

"This is perfect for now." Cameron leaned in. "The rooms at the inn are so luxurious. We have massages scheduled for tomorrow and in the afternoon we're going to the hot springs."

"Don't forget to stop by Ambrosia's crystal shop too. You'll enjoy that," Jill suggested.

"It's on my list. Jaclyn told us at trivia last week that she heard it's a must-see shop. She believes that crystals have magical healing properties."

"We play trivia almost every week at the River's End Ranch," Ethan explained. "Jaclyn is an older woman who plays with us and she seems to know everyone in this area."

"I heard about Ambrosia's shop too," Bethany said. "Maybe I'll stop in there soon too." She could pick up a healing crystal for her mother.

"If you like trivia, we could try our hand at music bingo," Jill suggested. "It's like trivia sort of, but all music related. You guess the name of the song after hearing a few notes. It's actually a lot of fun."

"Oh, I'd love to do that. What do you think, Ethan?" Cameron sounded excited.

"Sure. Sounds fun," he agreed.

"It will be starting in a few minutes. I saw Eddie handing out score sheets. I'll try to flag him down." She got his attention and a few minutes later, they joined a dozen or so teams as the game began.

Bethany ordered a glass of chardonnay when their waitress, Ivy, came by. She was Ryder's youngest sister and was humming along to the song they were supposed to guess the name of as she set her glass of wine down. It sounded so familiar, but they were all struggling to recall the name. Ivy looked as though she knew it. Suddenly it came to Bethany.

"Is it Landslide, by Stevie Nicks?" she asked her.

Ivy grinned. "That would be my guess."

Bethany conferred with the others and they agreed that it was their best guess. While they waited to hear the answer, she saw a familiar face at the bar. Ryder was just settling into an empty seat and Maggie was laughing as she slid a draft beer his way. He took a sip and slowly looked around the room, stopping when he saw her sitting at Jill's table.

He looked surprised to see her and lifted his glass. She nodded and smiled for a moment before turning her attention back to the others. Just a look from Ryder could still fluster her. And it didn't escape Jill's attention.

"Is that Ryder at the bar? Why don't you invite him to join us?"

"I don't want to bother him. He's chatting with Maggie."

"Who's Ryder?" Cameron asked.

"Ryder Quinn is one of the owner's of the restaurant. And he's Bethany's ex."

Cameron raised her eyebrows. "How interesting! And now you work here. How is that going?"

"It's fine. And it was a million years ago that we dated. Another lifetime."

"So, you're friends then. You could still invite him over. He looks so alone at the bar," Cameron said.

Maybe she should reach out and ask Ryder to join them. She'd like it if they could be good friends again at least. She was about to get up when Ethan spoke, "It doesn't look like he's alone anymore."

Sure enough, a tall, woman with gorgeous long blonde hair settled into the empty seat next to Ryder. Bethany couldn't see her face until she turned slightly and then her jaw dropped. It was Natalie Palmer. And her hand was on Ryder's arm as she leaned in to talk to him. A moment later, they were both laughing and Bethany was feeling a bit foolish to have assumed that he wasn't involved with anyone.

Jill raised her eyebrows. "Well, that didn't take her long."

"What do you mean?" Bethany took a sip of wine. The chardonnay was rich and creamy.

"Natalie's divorce was just finalized a week or so ago. She's always had a thing for Ryder."

"Oh, they're not a couple?"

Jill laughed. "They were for two seconds years ago. But it looks like Natalie wants to try again."

Bethany glanced over to the bar where Ryder was leaning back in his chair and looked amused by whatever Natalie was going on about. She was still a beautiful girl, and he looked like he was enjoying her company.

"Maybe he does too," Bethany said. Though the idea of it bothered her more than she was willing to admit.

CHAPTER 5

The next morning, on her way to the restaurant, Bethany drove to the far end of Main street to Ambrosia's crystal shop which was on the first floor of an old Victorian home. It was hard to miss because it was painted a pale purple and had scalloped gingerbread trim. A large bay window filled with crystals and jewelry twinkled as the sunlight fell upon it.

When Bethany opened the front door, soft chimes rang and Ambrosia looked up from the counter where she was sitting and thumbing through a book. A chipped tea cup sat by her side. The faint smell of lavender incense danced across the room. Ambrosia smiled and her face lit up. She stood and stepped out from behind the counter, ready to help. She was a pretty woman, maybe around thirty-five or so, Bethany guessed. She was wearing a gorgeous long, flowing ivory sweater over a purple and blue print skirt that swirled around her ankles.

"Welcome. Are you looking for anything in particular? Let me guess, you've lost a ring or something and you need some guidance to find it?"

Bethany guessed that she probably had a lost look about her as she knew very little about crystals. But, she had heard that they had healing properties and her mother could use all the help she could get.

She smiled. "No, I haven't lost anything. My mother just finished a round of chemotherapy and radiation. Can you suggest a stone or crystal that might help with her healing?" It sounded a bit crazy as she said it out loud, but Ambrosia nodded.

"I'm very sorry that your mother has been sick. I do have a few crystals that I would suggest." She led her over to an area filled with crystals of all sizes and colors. She carefully picked out three stones and handed them to Bethany one by one. The first was a pretty green color.

"Malachite. It helps with all forms of cancer and strengthens the immune system."

Bethany ran her hand over the stone, it felt cool and smooth.

"And this is Smoky Quartz. The darker the color the better. It is especially helpful with the after effects of chemotherapy." She dropped the coffee-colored crystal into Bethany's palm.

"Lastly, Yellow Kunzite helps with healing after radiation. It helps to strengthen the cells." This crystal almost seemed to glow from within. The color was like pale yellow light.

"Do you know how to use the crystals?" Ambrosia asked.

"No. I'm really not sure." Bethany had no idea what to do next.

Ambrosia smiled. "There's no one correct way, but you want to cleanse your crystals before using them and recharge them for at least four hours by setting them in either sunlight or moonlight. Whichever you prefer. Then you gather your stones close to you and you think about what you want them to do. It's really that simple."

"How do I cleanse them?"

"Wave them through a cleansing incense. This one is good." Ambrosia plucked a box of incense off a shelf and handed it to Bethany. "And once the stone is cleansed, some believe that the fairy inside will speak to you if you are deemed worthy." Ambrosia seemed to be waiting for some kind of a reaction from Bethany, but the comment left her speechless. *Fairies?*

"Let me get you a little pouch for your stones." Ambrosia led the way to the register and pulled a pale silvery blue velvet pouch with a silk drawstring from a drawer and held it open so Bethany could drop the crystals into it.

"Is there anything else I can get for you?" she asked.

"No, I think that's all I need."

"Hmmmm. Hold please." She wandered off to the

far corner of the room and came back a moment later with a pretty pink stone. "This one is with my compliments. Rose Quartz. You need it."

"I do? What is it for?"

Ambrosia smiled. "It's for giving the heart the love it deserves. It will bring positive energy into your life. Trust me."

It sounded silly to Bethany, but it was sweet of Ambrosia to give her the stone. "Thank you. That's very kind of you."

"Make sure you do the same process with this stone that I told you to do with your mother's. Once it's recharged, hold it close and keep it near you. By your bedside is a good spot."

"I'll do that. Thanks, Ambrosia."

When Bethany got home from work that evening, her mother and cat were in their usual spots. Her mother was reading a novel for her book club and Simon was kneading a blanket and purring so loudly that Bethany could hear him from across the room. They both looked up when she walked in.

"You're home early." Her mother closed the book and set it on the coffee table.

"It was slow tonight."

Her mother frowned. "I've heard that Quinn's isn't as busy as it used to be. I hope for their sake and for yours that they are doing ok?"

Bethany had the same concern. The pub had been busy the night before for music bingo but it had been very slow the next day for lunch and dinner. So slow that as much as she hated to do it, she was planning to talk to Ryder about it when she went in. She knew about the issues they'd had with the old chef but thought it was just about him stealing. It seemed as though business itself was down and she wondered what Ryder's plans were to turn things around.

"I'm going to talk to Ryder tomorrow and see what they have planned for marketing. People seem to love the new food."

"It might just take a while until word gets out that there's a new chef," her mother said.

"I agree. So, are you up for a smoothie?"

"Yes, I'd love one. I had your shepherd's pie for dinner, honey and it was excellent. You do comfort food well."

Bethany smiled. "Thank you. I'm glad you liked it. I'll be right back."

She returned a few minutes later with their green smoothies, handed one to her mother and settled onto the love seat.

"I stopped at Ambrosia's shop today. Have you ever been there?"

"With the crystals? No, I haven't. But I've always been curious about that place. Did you get anything?"

Bethany pulled the little pouch out of the bag Ambrosia had given her. She handed it to her mother.

"What's this?" She looked intrigued as she took the little pouch and peeked inside.

"Three crystals, for you. They're to help with your healing."

Her mother looked touched and curious. "Really? Thank you. How does it work?" She poured the crystals into her hand and held them up to the light. "They're so pretty."

Bethany explained what Ambrosia had shared about how to start using the crystals.

"We can start the process tonight. I bought the incense too. And I have a stone of my own."

"You do? What is yours for?"

Bethany hesitated for a moment. "For bringing positive energy into my life."

"Oh, that sounds lovely."

After they finished their smoothies. Bethany lit a stick of incense and waved it around the room and around their crystals. They took the crystals outside and set them on the front steps where the moonlight shone down upon them.

"They have to stay in the light for at least four hours. So we can just collect them in the morning."

"Perfect. We can gather them close and think happy thoughts while we have our morning coffee."

Bethany smiled. "That sounds like a good plan"

CHAPTER 6

Bethany arrived earlier than usual the next day. She was hoping to catch Ryder alone before the rest of the staff arrived so she could have a serious conversation with him about the financial health of the restaurant. She was admittedly a bit nervous to ask such sensitive questions, so she'd baked another batch of zen muffins, going even heavier on the lavender and ginger to help put Ryder in a more receptive mood. She'd noticed that he'd eaten every last crumb of the last batch she'd brought in, as had the rest of the family.

His door was ajar as she approached it and lightly knocked.

"Come in."

She stepped inside and was dismayed to see his mother and sister already there too, sipping coffee and all looking quite serious.

"I'm sorry, I didn't mean to interrupt anything,"

Bethany said and took a step backwards while Ryder and Maggie exchanged glances. Finally, his mother broke the ice by reaching for a muffin.

"So thoughtful of you dear to bring more of these delicious treats in for us. Why don't you have a seat and join us?"

"Are you sure that's a good idea?" Maggie said.

"Yes, I'm sure. Bethany is the chef here, she should know more about what's going on."

Ryder sighed. "You're right. Bethany, please pull up a chair and thank you for bringing muffins. Are these the same ones you made before?"

She smiled. "Yes, these are my zen muffins. I tweaked the recipe a little."

Both Ryder and Maggie eagerly reached for a muffin. Bethany had already had one, so she just sat sipping her coffee and wondering what they'd been discussing.

"You haven't really missed anything yet," his mother said. "Ryder was just going over the monthly numbers and projected forecasts for the coming weeks. We're a little below where we'd like to be."

"That's an understatement," Maggie said.

Ryder looked up from his spreadsheets and met her gaze straight on. "Our sales are down, way down from where they used to be. Gary, our old chef, had let things slide and we've lost some of our customers to other restaurants in the area."

"But now that Bethany's here, they'll come back," his mother said. She didn't seem overly concerned. But both Ryder and Maggie looked worried and Bethany didn't blame them. She'd seen more than one place have to close during a slowdown when they couldn't keep up with the daily expenses of running a restaurant.

"Bethany has only been here for a week. It may take a while before word gets out that the food here is really good again," Ryder said. He ran a hand through his hair and kept tapping a finger against his papers. It was a nervous habit she remembered from when they used to date. He got fidgety when he was stressed out.

"Are you open to suggestions?" she asked quietly.

"Why, have you run a restaurant before?" Ryder snapped.

"Ryder...." His mother cautioned.

He sighed. "I'm sorry. Yes, of course we're open to any suggestions."

"Well, I haven't run a restaurant before, but I was always involved in these kinds of meetings and I have seen a few things that worked to get the word out and turn things around. Do you do any advertising?"

"We have a radio ad that runs every weekend and a display ad in the weekly paper."

"Okay, and I'm guessing your budget is fully allocated?"

He laughed. "There's no extra money, if that's what you mean."

"That's what I figured. I'd suggest making a few changes, if you are open to them. I'd stop the radio ads and I'd put that money into printing coupons that you can give to area hotels for money off their meal, maybe $5 off or something like that. And I'd change your newspaper ads to highlight daily deal specials, like burger Wednesday and Prime Rib Thursday. That kind of thing."

"You want us to switch from radio ads to coupons?" Ryder looked skeptical.

"Radio is expensive and you might see a better ROI from the coupons. People that stay at the inn will be looking for places to dine and that discount will get them in the door."

"I like the idea of the daily deals. Comfort food classics that are family friendly cheap eats," his mother said.

"Exactly. Both of these things have worked really well for some of the places I've worked at."

"It's worth a shot, maybe. And it won't cost us any more than we're already spending," Maggie said.

"Okay, we can try it out. Thank you." Ryder reached for a second muffin and Bethany was happy to see that he seemed to be in a better mood already. "Oh, what was it you were coming to see me about?"

Bethany smiled. "This actually. I just wanted to learn more about how the restaurant was doing."

His mother reached for another muffin and smiled. "We're doing much better now that you're here, dear."

Maggie turned at the sound of the front door opening. "I think that's my liquor delivery. I'll catch up with you all later."

His mother stood and stretched. "I should be on my way as well."

"Where are you off to?" Ryder asked.

"I'm going to visit with Bethany's mother for a bit. She invited me over for tea."

Ryder looked as surprised as Bethany felt.

"I didn't realize that you two were friendly," he said. Bethany didn't either but kept quiet, curious to hear what his mother would say.

"We've been friends for a number of years now. We're also in the same book club. Bonnie hasn't been up to going lately, so we're going to chat about the book and anything else we feel like gossiping about."

Ryder smiled. "Well, have fun then, and please give her my regards."

"I'll do that. And Ryder, get on that advertising stuff today. I never did like that radio commercial much."

He grinned. "I never did either."

AFTER THE LUNCH RUSH DIED DOWN, RYDER visited with Maggie at the bar while she restocked and got the bar ready for the evening shift. She had the night off and was going out with friends to the other pub in town, O'Shea's, where Ivy was going to be singing with a friend's band. It was her first time playing there, and she was a little nervous. Maggie wanted to go and support her and tried to recruit Ryder too.

"So, you'll come by, at least for the last set? They'll probably go on again around nine."

"I should be able to manage that. Mom called earlier too, to remind me." Ryder stayed until closing most nights, but he really didn't have to. His assistant manager, Paul, was more than capable of closing things down. Ryder just usually liked to do it himself, especially after what happened with Gary and Suzanne.

He was pouring himself a glass of water when he noticed an older man about his mother's age walking toward them.

"You must be Ryder? And Maggie?" He glanced at his sister and Ryder tried to place him, but he had no idea who the man was.

"Yes, and you are?"

"Harry. Harry Peterman. I'm actually here to see your mother. Is she in?"

Maggie raised her eyebrows. It was clear that she had no idea who the guy was either.

"No. She's not. I can tell her you came by though."

"Oh dear. I was hoping she'd be in. Yes, of course. Let me give you a card. He fished in his pocket and drew out a thick ivory business card. It had his name and his business, Peterman Productions. Whatever that was.

"Please ask her to call me. It's been many years since I've seen her, but at one time we had a strong friendship. I've just recently moved back to the area."

"I'll let her know as soon as I see her," Ryder said.

As soon as the door closed behind him, Maggie spoke. "What was that about? Did mom have some kind of mystery life that we never knew about? What do you suppose Peterman Productions is?"

Ryder shook his head. "I have no idea. Funny that he knew our names though."

Maggie looked thoughtful. "Right. He must be an old friend or something." A mischievous look crossed her face. "Speaking of old friends. I noticed you and Natalie Palmer were chatting up a storm last night. Anything brewing there?"

"With Natalie? No."

"Well, she's single now, and available. She looked as though she wouldn't mind."

"Natalie is just lonely and recently divorced. She's a sweet girl." He'd always been fond of her.

"She's gorgeous too."

"I suppose." As pretty as Natalie was, she wasn't his type. Natalie was glamorous and turned heads wherever she went. Ryder preferred a softer, quieter beauty.

"You should take her on a date. See if there are any sparks there."

Maggie didn't usually push this hard. "Why do you care if I date Natalie?"

"Oh, I just thought she might be good for you. You were giving me a hard time, but truth is you haven't dated anyone seriously in a long time either."

Since Bethany.

"Natalie's not my type."

"Who is then? Bethany?" and there it was. Maggie was worried that he might try to get back together with Bethany.

"I take it you wouldn't approve?"

Maggie glared at him for a moment, her lips pressed in a thin line. Finally, she sighed. "No. I wouldn't. I saw what it did to you the last time she went away. I don't want to see that happen again. Do you really think she's not going to run back to New York as soon as her mother is healthy again?"

"She says she's not, but I don't really know. There's not much here for her."

"No, there's not," Maggie agreed. "I'd hate to see you hurt again, that's all."

He and Maggie were super close, and he appreciated her concern.

"You don't have to worry about me. I'm keeping my distance."

"Good." She poured herself a glass of diet soda and took a big sip. "So, we'll see you sometime between eight and nine?"

"I'll be there."

CHAPTER 7

G ood night, Ryder," Bethany said as she walked past his office on her way home. It was a quarter to eight, and she was tired. It had been a long day.

"Bethany, hold on a minute." Ryder closed his office door behind him and had his jacket on. "I'll walk out with you."

As they stepped outside he turned to her and asked, "Do you have plans or were you just heading home?"

"No plans. Why?"

"Ivy's playing at O'Shea's for the first time. I told her I'd go to support her. Maggie's already there with some friends. Do you want to come along?"

Ivy had mentioned to them the night before that she was going to be playing tonight and was excited about it.

"Sure. I can go for one drink. I don't want to be out too late though."

"It won't be a late night for me either. I just want to catch one of her sets. "

"Perfect, I'll meet you there then."

Bethany was still smiling as she got into her car and drove the short distance across town to O'Sheas's. Ryder seemed to be warming up to having her around and she was hopeful that they could maybe be friends again. She could use a friend here in Quinn Valley. Aside from Jill, she'd lost touch with her old friends. Many had moved away or married young and were busy with their families.

She found a spot right in front of O'Shea's and walked inside. Ryder was waiting for her and led the way through the bar to where Maggie and her friends had a big table near the stage. Maggie waved when she saw them and looked surprised to see Bethany with Ryder. Bethany hoped she didn't mind that Ryder had asked her to come along.

She used to really like Maggie, but since she'd started at the restaurant, Ryder's sister hadn't been all that friendly towards her. She knew that Ryder and Maggie weren't just co-owners of Quinn's Pub, they'd always been close and she guessed that Maggie was being protective of Ryder. But still, it didn't make her feel great.

Though when they reached the table, Maggie smiled and made room for them to slide in and take the two empty seats. She seemed to be in an unusually good mood.

"Thanks for coming. Ivy's more nervous than usual about this gig. She usually plays at smaller places."

Bethany looked around the room. O'Shea's had a much bigger bar area than Quinn's. The room was packed, and the crowd was all ages. The environment was a bit more casual. There were lots of young people in their twenties playing darts or pool while what looked like a group of regulars in their fifties were laughing and eating burgers at the bar. O'Shea's was an Irish bar. The Irish flag was proudly displayed along with the American one and there were paintings of Guinness beer on the wall and Irish music played in the background.

"Sally, I'll have another draft beer and these two probably want something," Maggie said to their very Irish-looking waitress. Sally had black hair, blue eyes and a spattering of freckles. She was also one of Maggie's best friends.

"I'll take a Guinness draft too, what do you want Bethany?" Ryder asked.

"Chardonnay please."

Sally went off to the bar and returned a few minutes later with their drinks.

It looked like Ivy would be on soon. There were two other guys in the small band and they were checking their equipment.

Bethany took a sip of her wine and noticed that Maggie was deep in conversation with her friends.

There were four of them and she'd been introduced, but the names had gone in one ear and out the other. Maggie was two years younger than her and all of her friends were from high school. They'd all stayed in Quinn Valley after going to college. The town was growing, and she was glad to see everyone doing well. Ryder looked deep in thought as he lifted his beer.

"I'm looking forward to hearing Ivy sing," she said.

"Oh, she's great. Really talented. She'd probably do well to leave Quinn Valley to be honest. Like you did." He didn't look happy at the idea.

"I didn't want to leave, you know. But, I felt like I had to," she said softly. She still felt a little guilty for leaving even though she knew she'd make the same choice again.

"I know. I was angry with you for a long time," he admitted. "It took me a long time to get over you."

"It took me a long time too."

They were both quiet for a moment and then Ryder said, "I was so surprised to see you that morning. I had no idea that you were back in town. You didn't come back often."

"No, I didn't. I came when I could, but you know how it is in the restaurant business. It's hard to take more than a few days at a time."

He grinned. "Yeah, I know. What was it like, working in Manhattan?"

"It was an adventure. Magical, wonderful and sometimes maddening." She paused to take a sip of her wine before continuing. "Culinary school in Vermont was such a special time and several summer co-ops on Nantucket and in Manhattan led to my first full-time position after graduating. I've worked at some incredible restaurants, cutting edge places as well as established icons. I learned a lot."

"It must seem so slow and ordinary here compared to that."

"It's nothing like Manhattan, but that's what I love about it. This is home. I always knew I'd come back, when the time was right."

"You weren't planning to come back this soon though?"

He was right about that. "Well, no. Not just yet. I thought probably in another year or so. But, I think things happen for a reason sometimes. I lost my job two weeks before I found out my mother was sick. I would have come immediately anyway, but it meant I could stay as long as I liked and the more I thought about it, I started to realize that I didn't need or want to go back."

"What would you have done if we didn't hire you?"

"I would have found something. There are lots of restaurants in Lewiston. I wouldn't like the commute, but I could do it if I had to. Or I might have tried to start up my own catering business. That's something I'd thought about too."

"Oh? What would that look like? Would you want to do weddings? That's a big undertaking."

"I know. And not really what I had in mind. I was thinking more personal chef type of thing. Dinner parties and to-go meals. I could imagine a small shop full of prepared meals that people could pick up and heat and eat when they got home."

"That's a really good idea, actually." Ryder looked thoughtful and Bethany thought he was about to say something but stopped when the music started and Ivy stepped up to the microphone. It was too loud to talk, so they sat back and listened. It was the first time that Bethany had heard Ivy sing and she was impressed.

They played a popular mix of covers, country as well as pop rock and some classics. Ivy had a way of singing that drew people's attention. The whole room seemed to focus on her. The last song she sang was an original song, and it was hauntingly beautiful. When she finished, the room was silent and then erupted in applause and cheers.

"She's really good," Bethany said.

"Yeah, she keeps getting better. I hadn't heard that last one before."

Maggie leaned their way. "She's amazing, huh? I keep telling her she should go to Nashville."

"Yeah, she probably should," Ryder agreed, but he didn't look thrilled at the idea. Bethany knew he wanted what was best for his sister and just hated the thought of her moving. He was a homebody and always had been. But now that she was older, Bethany could see both sides better. She knew it must have been hard for her mother for her to be so far away. They'd always been close and talked every few days. But since she'd been home, they'd grown even closer and Bethany couldn't even think about the possibility of her not overcoming her cancer.

"I should probably get going," Bethany said as she took the last sip of her wine and pulled out some money to put toward the bill. But, Ryder handed it back to her.

"I've got this." He handed some cash to Maggie and stood up. "I'll walk you to your car. I'm going to head home too."

"Thank you."

They said their goodbyes to Maggie and her friends and congratulated Ivy on the way out.

"You were amazing," Bethany said.

"Oh my gosh, thanks so much for coming."

"That last song was your best yet," Ryder told her and she looked thrilled by the compliment.

"Thank you. See you both tomorrow!"

When they reached Bethany's car, she took him by surprise by pulling him in for a hug. "Thank you for inviting me out. It was good to talk and just have fun."

"Yeah, it was good catching up with you. And fun. We might have to do it again sometime." He grinned.

"See you tomorrow, Ryder."

BETHANY WAS STILL SMILING AS SHE PULLED INTO the driveway. She was relieved that she and Ryder seemed to be in a better, friendlier place. And it wasn't too late, just a little after nine. Her mother should still be up so they could hang out a little before she went to bed.

When she walked in, her mother was in her usual spot, but her eyes were closed and she was holding the pouch of crystals against her chest while one of Simon's paws rested on her shoulder. She looked sound asleep but even though Bethany closed the door softly behind her, her mother's eyes fluttered open at the sound.

"Bethany, is that you?" she sat up a little and looked around the room.

"Hi, Mom. Sorry that I woke you."

"Oh, don't be silly. I was just resting my eyes for a minute."

"Can I get you anything? I'm going to make a cup of herbal tea."

"If it's not too much trouble, I'll have one of your green drinks. I think I'm addicted to them now."

Bethany laughed. "That's a good addiction!"

While her water was heating, she juiced a smoothie for her mother and brought the drinks back to the living room.

"Thanks, honey. Did you have fun at O'Shea's?"

"How did you know that's where I went?"

"Oh, I just assumed. Marcia mentioned this morning when she came over that Ivy was playing tonight. She was going to suggest that Ryder invite you. She knew Maggie was going too. David and Carter would have gone, but they were at some industry event." Hmmm, so it wasn't necessarily all Ryder's idea to invite her. Still, he didn't have to agree, and they'd had a good time.

"I didn't realize you and Marcia had become good friends."

"She's been wonderful since I've been sick. All my friends have really. Marcia is easy to spend time with and now that she's retired, she has more time to visit. She likes to come a few mornings a week for tea after she stops by the restaurant.

"I see you're trying out the crystals."

"Oh, yes. I did just what you said earlier. I held them in both hands and focused on thinking about healing. And then I felt so relaxed that I must have drifted off to sleep. Hopefully that's a good sign that they're working?"

She was so enthusiastic. Bethany had always loved that about her. Her mother was the most positive person she knew. And she had a good feeling about those crystals and her mother's cancer. She'd been eating well since Bethany came home and was due for a followup visit the next week. Her color looked better, and they were both hopeful that her numbers would show improvement too.

"I think it's a very good sign," Bethany agreed.

LATER, WHEN SHE WENT TO BED, BETHANY PICKED up the pretty pink rose quartz crystal and held it in both of her hands. She closed her eyes and let her mind drift. The stone felt warm as she focused on wishing for positive energy for herself, her mother and for Ryder and the restaurant. She wanted it to do better for all of their sakes. After a few minutes, she set the crystal on her nightstand and slid into bed. She felt relaxed and content as she drifted off to sleep.

CHAPTER 8

Ryder was in a good mood the next morning as he sat drinking coffee at the bar with his brothers. Both David and Carter had stopped in for a quick visit as they knew their mother would be there too. Maggie, Ivy and Bethany would be arriving any minute.

"So, Ivy was good last night, huh? I was sorry to have missed it," David said.

"She was great. We all thought so."

"Who went?" Carter asked.

"Me, Maggie, a bunch of her friends and Bethany." His brothers exchanged glances while his mother just smiled and sipped her tea. He knew if their mother wasn't sitting there that one of both of them would have asked more questions. He was grateful that she was there because he wasn't ready to answer them. He just knew that he'd had a better time than he'd imagined with Bethany.

It had been good to talk, really talk to her and it felt comfortable, almost like it used to feel. She'd always been easy to talk to. And when she surprised him with that hug at the end of the night, he'd been blown away by how right it had felt and how familiar.

He'd inhaled her sweet scent and wanted to hold on longer. Bethany had always felt like home to him, which is why it was so devastating when she left. He understood why she went though. He hadn't understood at first though.

"Don't forget about the tasting event Friday afternoon," David reminded him as Bethany walked in.

"Come have coffee with us, dear," his mother called her over.

Bethany slid into the chair next to her and took a sip from the coffee she'd brought with her, from Fresh Brew, the takeout coffee shop down the street.

"You should bring Bethany with you," David suggested.

"Oh, that's a marvelous idea!" his mother agreed.

"She can taste our new meats," Carter added.

"What are you talking about?" Bethany looked confused.

"We are having our annual tasting. It's when we invite all of our clients in to sample products from our vendors. It's a great way to try what's new."

"Oh, those are always fun. But what time is it? I might not be able to go."

"It's Friday afternoon from two to five."

"That's during the slow time," his mother said.

"Tom can cover for you if necessary. And I can always pop in too. I'm just a phone call away."

Ryder chuckled. "It sounds like it's settled then. Bethany will join me Friday afternoon." He found himself looking forward to the event more than he usually did.

"I'm looking forward to it," Bethany said.

Ryder realized he'd forgotten to do something. He pulled out his wallet and found the thick business card he'd put there the day before and handed it to his mother.

"I almost forgot to tell you this. A Harry Peterman stopped by to see you yesterday. He was disappointed that you weren't here. He wants you to give him a call."

He watched as his mothers fingers shook as she took the card and looked at it. She gazed out the window for a moment and then back at them.

"I thought I saw him the other day. He was just walking along the street and stopped for a minute by the bay window. I was sure that I imagined it. He's been gone for so long."

"Who is he?" Ryder asked.

"He's a very old, dear friend. I knew him before I met your father. We were high-school sweethearts. But his family moved away during our senior year. We kept in touch for a while, but he had big dreams. I knew he wasn't coming back to Quinn Valley any time soon."

"What is Peterman Productions?" Ryder was curious about what he'd read on the card.

"I'm not really sure. Harry had always loved

theater and movies. His dream was to do something with film."

"Are you going to call him?" David asked.

"Of course I am. It would be rude not to!"

THE REST OF THE WEEK FLEW BY AND BEFORE Bethany knew it, Friday afternoon had arrived and it was time to go to the tasting event with Ryder. They'd had a very busy lunch which was both wonderful and concerning as she didn't want to leave if it was still really busy. But by one thirty, the rush was over and only a few customers were still there. She'd be coming back for the dinner service but it would be nice to get out for a few hours.

"Are you ready to go?" Ryder walked into the kitchen, wearing his jacket.

"Just about." Bethany slipped off her white chef coat and hung it on a hook by the door and pulled on her own jacket. "I'm ready."

She followed Ryder to his navy blue Honda CRV and climbed in the passenger side. She noticed a few boxes on the back seat as she buckled in.

"I picked those up from the printer this morning. I need to drop them off with Rachel at the Inn. She loved the idea of discount coupons. Said it was another great perk they could offer their guests." Rachel was the assistant manager there. It was a big job but according to Marcia, who had just mentioned her a few days ago, Rachel was doing a fabulous job.

"That's great. Do we have time to drop them off on our way? Then maybe they could start giving them out this weekend."

Ryder checked his watch. "We go right by there, so we can make a quick stop."

Five minutes later, he pulled up to the valet station in front of the main entrance. A young man came rushing over and smiled when he saw Ryder.

"Hey, Dylan. Can we just leave the car here for a minute while we drop a few boxes off?"

"Of course. I'll keep an eye on her for you."

There were two boxes in the back seat. Ryder grabbed the bigger one and Bethany picked up the smaller one. It wasn't heavy, just a little bulky. When they walked in the front door, Rachel was coming their way and looked surprised to see them.

"Hey, Ryder. I didn't think I'd see you until tomorrow."

"We were coming this way anyway, so I thought we'd go ahead and drop the coupons off."

"Well, that's great. Follow me." She led them into her office and told them to set the boxes on the floor. She reached in and pulled out a stack of coupons and smiled.

"I'll bring these up to the front desk now. We'll put some in our tourist attractions room, where guests can browse brochures of all the local sights. And I'll make sure that every guest that checks in from now on gets two coupons."

"Thanks, Rachel. I really appreciate it," Ryder said.

"It's a fantastic idea, and it's something we can give to our guests. I really think they're going to love it."

"I wish I could say it was my idea, but it was all Bethany's."

Rachel looked at her with interest. "Really? I heard you've been working in Manhattan. Did they use coupons like this there?"

"Yes. And in Nantucket too when I spent a summer there. Tourists love a good deal."

"Keep me posted how it goes," Rachel said

"I will. We're off to David's annual tasting event now."

"That's today? I think I was supposed to go to that too. Maybe I can sneak out a little later."

"It goes until five I think," Ryder told her. They said their goodbyes and ten minutes later pulled up to David's giant warehouse.

"Wow," Bethany said. It looked like quite an operation.

"David has done well for himself."

"It looks like he has enough food to serve most of Idaho in there."

Ryder laughed. "Every year he expands. He has trucks that go to Riston, Lewiston, and beyond."

He parked, and they made their way inside. As soon as David saw them he came over and gave

Bethany a tour. He seemed to carry just about everything a restaurant could need.When they came back to the main room where the tasting was being held, he gave them both a printout that listed all the attending vendors and what they were going to be sampling.

"I hope you're both hungry?"

Bethany nodded. She was actually starving. Normally she would have eaten something once the lunch rush started to slow, but she hadn't had anything since breakfast.

"Good. I'd start with Bella Cheese, their baby fresh mozzarella balls dipped in oil and balsamic glaze are a hit."

Bethany headed straight there and happily popped one in her mouth. They were as delicious as David had said. Ryder agreed, and they spent the next hour strolling around the room, chatting with the various vendors who were all friendly and interested in learning about Quinn's Pub and how their products could fit in there. There were quite a few things they tasted that impressed them both and Bethany's mind whirled as she imagined different ways to serve the various foods she'd tasted.

They spent quite a bit of time with Carter as he explained to Bethany all about what he did and the various humanely raised and organic meats he sold. She tasted everything and the quality and freshness rivaled the best meats she'd had in Manhattan and she told him so.

"I believe in our quality, but I have to say it made

my day to hear that. Thank you." He told them about some new products he hoped to have in the coming year before they made their way to the final table which was desserts. Although every restaurant Bethany had worked at made some of their own desserts, almost every one bought some too. And desserts was one area that she thought they could improve on at Quinn's.

They tried small bites of at least a dozen different desserts—everything from cheesecakes to rich chocolate layer cakes to fancy pies and even a few frozen desserts. There were two that stood out to Bethany. A deceptively simple apple crisp that had toasted walnuts, oats, lots of brown sugar and butter and perfectly cooked apples. They served it with vanilla bean ice cream on top, which was how she would serve it too.

The other standout was the chocolate cake. It was six layers of rich decadence and she knew it was the kind of dessert that people would talk about. It was oversized and outrageous. And who didn't like chocolate cake?

It reminded her of one she'd had in Boston at Abe and Louie's. She'd gone there for lunch with a fellow student and before she even decided what she wanted to order, she'd seen three chocolate cakes go by and knew that was what she was having for dessert. It was magnificent. Almost as good as this one.

"You're in love," Ryder said with an amused smile.

"I am. And you will be too as soon as you take a

bite. We're ordering this today. The apple crisp too. This is exactly the kind of comfort food dessert that people are going to go crazy for. And it doesn't make sense for me to make it when they do it so well."

Ryder took a bite of the chocolate cake and while he was still swallowing gave it the thumbs up.

"I was thinking the cannoli until I tasted this. But you're right. This makes much more sense."

Bethany smiled. "Cannoli are delicious too but they are messy and get soggy too fast."

"It's hard to top the cannoli from the bakery down the street, anyway."

"That's true and we can always get them occasionally for a special. But this cake is going to be our signature dessert." Bethany was so enthusiastic that Ryder looked amused and just nodded in agreement.

"Whatever you want works for me. You're the expert."

David came over as they finished up.

"So, what do you think? See anything you want to add to the menu?"

Bethany and Ryder both laughed.

"Bethany wants to add a lot of things, I think. But we'll start with the chocolate cake and apple crisp," Ryder said.

"Great, I'll include some of both in your next order. Bethany can let me know when she wants to add some other items."

"Perfect," Ryder said.

As they drove back to the restaurant, Bethany

looked forward to getting the desserts on the menu and had a few new ideas for some of the other things she'd tasted. She was excited to see how their customers would respond.

When they parked and walked toward's Quinn's, Ryder asked, "So, are you glad you went?" He was smiling and she knew he was teasing her.

"So glad. Ryder, I really think we can turn things around for Quinn's."

She saw something warm and appreciative in his eyes. "I sure hope so."

CHAPTER 9

Quinn's was busier than usual Friday and Saturday night. David arranged for a delivery of the desserts they'd ordered for Saturday morning, so Bethany ran them as specials until they could get them added onto the new menus. They were still working on what the final changes to the menu would be. She wanted to test out a few things and see how customers responded before finalizing anything.

She was pleased to hear that some discount coupons were already being redeemed. They had a few trickle in on Friday and a steady flow of them Saturday night. She was also glad she'd suggested that Ryder accept them on weekends too, instead of just during the week as many restaurants did.

Feedback on both desserts was as she'd hoped. Customers loved both and particularly raved about the chocolate cake. Bethany had added her own touch to the decadent cakes-a sprinkling of crushed lavender. It was one of her favorite herbs and she thought it might help promote romantic feelings. The slices were so tall that most people ended up taking half of it home with them and the overall consensus was that they more than got their money's worth.

Bethany worked late both nights and let her assistant go home early, to give him a break. By the time she left each night, she was ready to fall into bed, but it was the good kind of tired, when she felt like she was making a difference. The energy in Quinn's was already different.

She sensed that slowly but surely, people were coming back, and were curious if they'd been away, to see if the new chef had made improvements. She heard from the servers that they loved the new dishes that she'd introduced. The chicken pot pie she ran as a special was so popular she'd added it to the regular menu, along with the short ribs and meatloaf.

Sunday and Monday were her days off and she wasn't used to having two full days off. Everywhere else she'd worked the chefs and sous chefs worked six and often seven days a week and usually from open to close. It was a punishing schedule and part of what had attracted her to the possibility of starting up her own catering business. She would work long hours no doubt, but she'd also have a flexible schedule. She was glad though that she didn't have to do that yet. The position at Quinn's seemed tailor made to her and the expected hours were more than reasonable.

She and her mother had a relaxing Sunday. Her mother wanted to get out of the house and go to an early church service, which wouldn't be as crowded. They both enjoyed the peacefulness of the small, quiet service. And her mother was happy to see some of her friends afterward at coffee hour.

They went for a walk when they got home as the weather was cool and clear. Her mother rested after that, curled up on the living room sofa with a book while Bethany puttered in the kitchen making a roasted chicken and vegetables. The house quickly smelled amazing, and she planned on making a chicken soup from the bones the next day. Bone broth was supposed to be extra nutritious and so far her mother's diet seemed to be helping.

They enjoyed a lazy afternoon together. Bethany also read for a while, a Melinda Leigh mystery that had her on the edge of her seat. And they both snacked on a frozen treat that she made. As an experiment, she froze one of her green smoothies as popsicles and they turned out better than expected.

She got a good night's sleep and met up with Jill the next day for lunch. It was a last minute invitation as Jill had a cancellation and was just going to walk next door and grab a salad. Bethany met her at Smith's and also ordered a salad. Jill always made her laugh with some of her funny stories about her patients. She never shared any identifying details of course, and Bethany wouldn't know them anyway, but it was still fun to hear them.

"I had a young couple that had their first baby delivered yesterday. The husband was in the delivery room. I told him that the baby's head was starting to crown and that it was time to push. He put on gloves and then stepped back and squatted as if he was preparing to catch a football! Everyone in the room laughed while I explained to him that babies don't get tossed out of the womb."

Bethany laughed. "He must have been so out of his element."

"He was. I heard he was a star quarterback in high school. It was probably instinctual for him."

As they finished eating, Bethany asked if Jill had plans the next night. "I'm meeting my mother and her friends after work at Quinn's for music bingo. It's my mother's first official night out since she finished her treatments."

"Oh, that's wonderful. I'd love to join you."

When they stepped outside, Bethany noticed a new shop a few doors down. At least it was new to her. "Have you been to there yet? It looks cute."

"Scentiments? Yes, I've been in there a few times. Their stuff smells amazing. They have all kinds of things made with essential oils. You should stop in. They haven't been open long, but Lindy, the woman that runs the shop is great and they're doing a good business."

"I will stop in there. I bet my mom would love a sweet smelling candle." She grinned. "Who am I kidding? I'd love one too."

Jill headed back to her office while Bethany walked down the street to the new shop. When she stepped inside a tangle of wonderful smells teased her nose. She was curious to learn more about essential oils as she thought she remembered hearing something about them being useful for healing too. A woman about her age looked up from behind the counter and smiled.

"Hi there, I'm Lindy. Can I help you find anything?"

Bethany hesitated. She wasn't really sure what she was looking for. "I was just curious to look around. I don't know much about essential oils, but my mother has breast cancer. Is there anything you might suggest?"

"Many people believe that there are a few essential oils that have some healing benefits for cancer. Frankincense, Myrrh, Lavender, Peppermint and especially, curcumin. You might know it as Turmeric."

"The yellow spice?" Bethany often used it to add a golden glow and subtle flavor to rice pilafs.

"That's the one. I have a collection of all five in small purse size vials. There's a pamphlet that explains each one. If she just dabs a little oil behind her ear or on her pulse points that's all she needs to do."

"Thank you." Bethany continued to wander around and selected a few candles as well as a lip balm for each of them.

"How long have you been here?" she asked as Lindy took her credit card and put everything in a pink shopping bag.

"I haven't been here long. Just about a week or so. It's actually my aunt's shop, but she hurt her back so I'm helping her out for a while." She handed Bethany her credit card slip and added with a smile, "I've always enjoyed helping her in the store. The essential oils are fascinating and seem to be helping so many people. I hope they help your mother."

"Thank you."

CHAPTER 10

Ryder was in an unusually good mood when he walked into the kitchen Tuesday afternoon. It was a little after two and Bethany was experimenting with a new green smoothie recipe.

"What are you making?" he asked as she flipped the blender switch on.

"I'm trying a new smoothie recipe. I've been making these green drinks for my mother. She's coming in tonight for music bingo with her friends and I wanted to have this for her. All her friends will be drinking alcohol. But this is much better for her."

"Can I try a taste?"

"Sure." She poured the smoothie into two plastic cups and handed one to him. He took a sip and looked surprised.

"This isn't bad at all. I thought it might be awful."

Bethany laughed. "I don't do awful. But it's missing

one key ingredient. I couldn't find lemongrass anywhere in Quinn Valley."

"Lemongrass, Hmmm. Let me think about that. It still tastes good without it."

"It does. But the lemongrass is a known cancer fighter and immune booster."

"I'll keep an eye out for some for you."

"Thank you."

"So, on another note, I just wanted to share that our receipts were up by over thirty percent this weekend. The coupons were a hit and the chocolate cake gives us a huge profit margin. That was a good call."

Bethany smiled. "Thanks. I'm glad to hear it."

"Well, I'm off to the bank and to run some errands. I'll be back before the dinner rush."

Bethany watched him go and was glad to see him in such a good mood. He seemed a little more relaxed than usual and she guessed that he'd been carrying around a lot of stress, worrying about the restaurant's financial situation.

"That's the first time I've seen Ryder smile like that in ages," Tom said. He was busy prepping pot pies and had overheard their conversation. "It was busier than it's been in a long time last night. I have to say, I much prefer working with you over Gary any day."

"Thanks, that's nice to hear." She liked Tom. He was young, but he was a talented cook and had some fun suggestions for their menu too.

"Your food is much better than his and you're a lot

nicer too. Gary was never interested in any of my ideas."

An order came into the kitchen which got his attention and he wandered off to the computer to see what it was. Bethany finished her smoothie and started thinking about the night's specials.

A little past four, Ryder came back into the kitchen holding a small plastic bag and wearing a smile. He handed the bag to Bethany. She peeked inside and her jaw dropped. It was filled with fresh lemongrass.

"Where did you find this?"

"Carter has an extensive herb garden as well as produce. I totally forgot to mention it to you, but he has everything you could imagine and said he could keep you well stocked with lemongrass if you want it."

Bethany felt her eyes water, she was overcome with gratitude and emotion. It was such a sweet, thoughtful gesture.

She nodded. "I'd love that. Thank you."

"Maybe you should try adding that smoothie as a special. People are really into nutrition these days, it might be a decent seller."

"It might. That's a great idea. Oh, and Ryder I'm joining my mother and her friends for music bingo when I finish up here. Jill is coming too. Would you like to join us?"

He looked surprised and pleased by the invitation. "I just might. Thanks."

At a quarter past seven, Bethany hung up her chef coat, fluffed her hair, and carried her mother's lemongrass kissed smoothie out to her table. They were sitting at a big round table. Bethany sat next to her mother and Jill was on the other side of her. Her mother's friends Glenda and Janie were also there, and they were all sharing a piece of the chocolate cake. Bethany smiled when she saw it.

"Hi honey," her mother said as she dug her fork into the cake. Bethany set her smoothie down and waved to Ryder who was looking around the room. When he reached their table, he sat in the empty seat beside her.

"Are you playing with us? We'll be unstoppable!" her mother exclaimed. She looked excited to be out and happy to see Ryder.

"Ryder found the lemongrass for your smoothie, mom," Bethany told her.

"Did you? Well, isn't that impressive? Thank you." She took a sip and pushed it toward Bethany. "Have you tried it? This is your best yet."

"I had some earlier. I'll take a bite of that cake though." She had a mouthful of chocolate cake when Ivy came over to get her drink order.

"I'll have that new draft IPA and I'm guessing Bethany wants a chardonnay?" Ryder said.

Bethany nodded, her mouth still full of cake. A moment later she thanked him.

They spent the next few hours laughing and trying to win at music bingo. It wasn't as easy as it seemed. Too often they all knew the song but none of them could remember the name of it. But somehow they managed to come in second. Her mother was just as thrilled as if they'd won first place.

Bethany suspected she was just happy to be out with her friends and glad to be feeling better. Her blonde hair was like peach fuzz, just starting to grow back. She left her head bare around the house, but when they went out, she usually wore a pretty scarf or a hat, or sometimes both. Tonight she had on a pink baseball cap and it made her look younger than her fifty-five years.

"That was so fun," she said as they paid their bill and got ready to leave. Glenda, Janie and Jill said their goodbyes and left. Bethany's mom wanted to use the ladies room first, so they waited for her to return and then Ryder walked them out. When they reached her mother's car, she suddenly slumped against it and grabbed Bethany's arm in a panic.

"Honey, I feel really funny all of a sudden." She went limp as Bethany grabbed hold of her to prevent her from falling.

"Did she faint?" Ryder asked.

"Yes, I'm not sure what's going on."

"Hold tight. I'll drive my car over and we can bring her to the ER."

Her mother was already starting to stir when Ryder pulled up. He jumped out and helped Bethany to get her into the back seat. They laid her down, so she wouldn't fall over if she fainted again.

Bethany got into the passenger seat and Ryder drove off toward the Riston hospital. It was on the outskirts of town, near the Quinn Valley line and there was no traffic so it took them less than twenty minutes to get there.

"Has she ever done this before?" Ryder asked as he pulled up to the front door and helped Bethany to get her mother out and into a wheelchair. There were a row of them, waiting outside for those who were too weak to walk.

"Yes, once, right after she started chemo. It knocked her socks off and she ended up in the ER. Her red blood cell count was low as a side effect of the treatment."

Bethany told the triage nurse about her mother's history and that she'd fainted before. They brought her right in and started running tests. Bethany and Ryder stayed with her in her area that had curtains for walls. Her mother was awake now, but weak and sleepy. She drifted off to sleep while they waited for the doctor to come.

When he walked over, both Bethany and Ryder recognized him. They'd graduated high school with Kevin Murphy. He'd been the class valedictorian and Bethany relaxed a little, knowing that her mother was in good hands.

"Hey, I know you two!" Kevin smiled and tried to put them both at ease. "Sorry to be running into you under this kind of circumstance though. What brings you all in?"

Since her mother was asleep, Bethany explained what had happened and her mother's history. "She's all done with treatments, both radiation and chemo-therapy and we're hopeful that it's worked. But, this doesn't seem like a good sign, does it?" Bethany bit her lip. She'd been worried sick the whole way there.

"Not necessarily. I see this often. It could just be a delayed reaction to the chemo. Your mom might be a little anemic again. We will get to the bottom of it though. We're going to run a bunch of tests and then figure out our next step. Sound good?"

"Thank you." Bethany stretched and glanced at her mother who was still sound asleep. Ryder reached out and massaged the back of her neck, kneading the tight muscles. It felt absolutely wonderful. She knew she'd been carrying a lot of tension there.

"Don't worry. Your mother's going to be fine. I know it."

Bethany forced a smile. "I feel better now that we're here. And she has Kevin for a doctor! Did you know he was a doctor?"

"I think I heard that years ago. It makes sense. He was always the smartest guy I knew."

"He was." She yawned and looked at the clock. It was already nine-thirty. "You don't have to wait with us, Ryder. We can get a cab home. It's probably going to be awhile."

"I'm not going anywhere. Except down to the cafe-teria to get a coffee. Do you want one?"

"I'd love a hot chocolate, actually."

"You got it."

While he was gone, nurses and other medical

people were in and out of the room, checking her mother's vital signs, drawing blood, and putting an IV in. Her mother woke up again briefly and fell fast asleep again once they were done poking and prodding her. By the time Ryder returned with her hot chocolate, the room was quiet again.

"Do you remember that time I broke my leg?" he asked as he settled back into his chair.

"Of course I remember." He broke it playing football during his senior year.

"You stayed with me the entire time in the hospital. I never forgot that." He looked around the room. "It's scary being here when something happens. Your mom could use the extra support."

"Thank you." Bethany took the top off her hot chocolate and blew on it to cool it a little. She took a tentative sip. It was still too hot to drink. She thought back to that day when she'd come to this hospital with Ryder. It had been terrifying for both of them. It had happened so fast, a normal play that had dangerous consequences.

He'd been rushed to the hospital and no one knew how bad it was at first as he'd passed out too, knocked unconscious. Bethany's mind had imagined the worst, brain damage, paralysis. When the doctor told them the verdict, a broken leg, they were all so relieved. His mother had cried happy tears. And Ryder had been so cranky. All he knew was that he was in a lot of pain and his football year was over.

It had brought them closer together though as they

spent even more time together once he wasn't going to football practice or games every week. She'd helped him to carry his books and they spent every afternoon together. It was nice to feel needed and useful. And loved. It was soon after the accident when Ryder first told her that he loved her and couldn't imagine not having her in his life.

He'd gotten so serious quickly after that and wanted to get engaged as soon as they both graduated from high school. Her mother was hesitant but supportive if that's what Bethany wanted to do. She knew then that she loved Ryder more than she'd imagined she could love anyone, but she also knew just as strongly that at nineteen she was too young to get married.

She'd told him then that she might be open to getting engaged but that it would be years before she'd be ready to get married. He was heading off to college and she still had culinary school to go to, and she knew she needed to work her way up in good restaurants where she'd have opportunities to learn from the best in the business. Waiting to get married seemed perfectly sensible to her.

But Ryder had felt very differently. He thought she was being selfish and that she obviously just didn't love him enough. She tried to explain over and over again but it fell on deaf ears. They were both upset and heartbroken at the time, but she knew now that he just wasn't mature enough to understand why she had to go and that it had nothing to do with not loving him.

"What are you thinking about?" Ryder asked softly.

She smiled. "Just remembering our senior year, your accident. It was awful but I think it brought us together more too."

"It did. You helped me get through a hard time. That's when I knew I was falling in love with you. And it's why it was so hard when you left," he added.

"I know. It was really hard leaving you too. You bounced back quickly enough though," she said.

His eyes narrowed. "What do you mean by that?"

"Well, I heard you started dating Natalie a week after I left for school."

He sighed. "We didn't date long. Natalie is a great girl, but she wasn't you. After I took her out a few times, I didn't date anyone for months."

"I saw her chatting with you at the bar last week. And I heard she's divorced now. You could have your second chance," she teased.

He stared at her intently for a moment and then shook his head. "I'm still not interested in Natalie."

Bethany wasn't sure what to say to that so she just sipped her hot chocolate.

"What about you? Is there anyone waiting for you in Manhattan?" Ryder asked casually.

The question made her laugh. "No. Hardly. I've had a few relationships over the years, but never anything long-term or serious. It's hard in our business, with the hours we work. I mostly dated other chefs or bartenders."

Kevin walked back over to them, carrying his clipboard and test results.

"So, we've run our tests and as I suspected, it looks like your mother is a little anemic. We're going to give her a blood transfusion which takes a few hours and then you'll be able to take her home soon after that. There's a waiting room if you want to relax and watch some TV while we give her the treatment.

Bethany watched as they wheeled her mother to the treatment room and then followed Ryder to the waiting room. There was a comedy playing, and they settled on the sofa to watch and wait. They chatted for a bit then got lost in the movie. Bethany felt her eyes grow heavy about half-way through and woke up a while later feeling disoriented. She was leaning against Ryder and his arm was around her. She sat up and looked at the time. Several hours had passed. Ryder was asleep too and stirred when she moved. She settled back against him and closed her eyes.

An hour or so later, Ryder was gently shaking her awake. "Bethany, your mother is all done. It's time to take her home."

Her mother was more awake than both of them when they returned to her area of the ER. Kevin was there going over her discharge orders.

"You should feel a lot better after this and have more energy. All of your other data was very good." He looked at Bethany. "Her white blood cell counts were actually improved by a lot. Whatever you're doing, keep it up."

An aide brought the wheelchair for her mother and she sniffed at it. "I don't need that thing. I'm perfectly capable of walking."

Kevin smiled at her. "Of course you are. But consider it part of the service. Save your strength for getting well."

"All right then." She eased herself into the wheelchair and Ryder wheeled her out to his car. They got her settled in the backseat and headed home. When they reached the house, Bethany and Ryder walked her mother inside.

"Ryder, thank you so much," her mother said and then surprised him with a hug. "I always did like you." She wandered off to her bedroom with Simon trailing behind her. Ryder looked exhausted. Bethany walked him to the door.

"Thanks a million. I'll see you in the morning."

Ryder smiled and his dimples stood out. "Good night, Bethany."

CHAPTER 11

Ryder was half-asleep when he walked into Fresh Brew to get a to-go coffee to bring into the restaurant. He stopped short when he saw a sight that he'd never seen before—his mother with a man that wasn't his father. It had been nearly ten years since they'd lost his father to a massive heart attack and his mother hadn't dated anyone or shown any interest in dating at all since. And now she was sitting and having coffee with Harry Peterman. They were laughing and so lost in their conversation that they didn't even notice him. He watched them curiously as he paid for his coffee and then had to walk right by them again on his way out.

This time his mother saw him and he hadn't seen her so happy in a long, long time.

"Ryder, come meet Harry!"

He stopped by their table and nodded. "Nice to see you again, Harry."

"Oh, that's right. I forgot that the two of you already met. Harry's moved back to Quinn Valley. Isn't that marvelous?"

"Sure, that's great. Where did you move from?"

"Hollywood. I worked in the movie business for many years. Still do actually, but now that everything is digital, I can do a lot of my work remotely."

"Harry is a film editor. He has a fancy studio at his house."

"You've seen it?" Ryder wasn't sure how he felt about his mother going to a strange man's house. Though he realized that Harry wasn't a stranger to her.

"No, not yet. But I will tonight. Harry's having me over for dinner. We have so much to catch up on."

"I'm not much of a cook, but I can order a mean pizza," Harry said.

"I love pizza." His mother was a little too enthusiastic for his liking.

"I have to get going. Have fun you two."

WHEN HE REACHED QUINN'S HE SAW THAT Bethany's car was already there. And when he walked in the kitchen to say hello, she was behind the line, making pie crust. She looked as exhausted as he felt.

"How's your mother doing?" he asked.

"Much better. I think she slept better than I did. I made her a smoothie and a spinach omelet before I left."

"For the iron?"

"Yes. I know it's silly as the transfusion took care of the anemia, but I figure it can't hurt to have her eat iron-rich foods too. Speaking of mothers, I haven't seen yours yet. She's usually here soon after I get in."

"I ran into her at the coffee shop. With a man." He told her about Harry Peterman and how he'd stopped by the restaurant a few days ago hoping to see his mother."

"And they were high school sweethearts before she met your father? How romantic that they'd find their way back to each other after all this time."

"I suppose. I just want her to be happy." He frowned. "I thought she was done with all that."

Bethany gave him a look. "With all what?"

"You know, romance."

She laughed. "Your mother is still young. I think it would be great if she could find love again."

His mother in love again. Ryder couldn't picture it.

"I'll be in my office, holler if you need anything."

BETHANY HAD SEVERAL CUPS OF COFFEE throughout the day, hoping a second wind would kick in. She'd gotten to bed so late the night before and slept badly. Fortunately the restaurant was too busy for her to think about how tired she was. And just before the dinner service, the caffeine finally kicked in and the next few hours flew by. She finished up at about a quarter to eight and when she left the kitchen and was going to head out the front door, Ryder waved her over. He was sitting at the bar chatting with Maggie.

"Have a quick drink with me?" He had a freshly poured beer in front of him and it suddenly looked good. Or maybe he looked good, who was she fooling?

"Okay, just one though." Maggie started pouring the chardonnay that she liked and set it down on the bar as Bethany settled into her seat.

"You always get the same thing, so I figured I was safe with this." Maggie smiled and Bethany sensed that her iciness was beginning to thaw. She liked friendly Maggie much more.

"Thank you."

"I was just telling Maggie about Mom and Harry."

"She hasn't been in at all today. That's a first," Maggie said.

"I'm happy for her." Bethany was curious to see how Maggie felt.

"Hmmmm. He didn't look like he belonged around here. How do we know he'll stick around?"

"We don't. But if he breaks our mother's heart, I'll just have to kill him." Ryder spoke with such seriousness that Bethany and Maggie stared at him until he started laughing and they joined in.

"It would be great for her if she found someone. She's still young," Maggie said.

"That's what I said earlier too," Bethany agreed.

"I have to run to the ladies room for a minute. Ryder can you keep an eye on the bar for me?"

"Sure thing."

As Bethany took a sip of wine a well-dressed couple walked in and took seats at the bar. She couldn't place him, but the man looked vaguely familiar. She noticed Ryder stiffen before he stood and went behind the bar to take their drink order. When he came back her way to pour a draft beer, his eyes were cold and his jaw was clenched. She glanced at the couple. The man was dark-haired and in a suit and the woman with him was in a stylish suit too. She was petite and blonde, with long, feathery hair and a huge diamond engagement ring. It sparkled when the overhead light hit it.

"That's Jason. The one that broke Maggie's heart. And he's already engaged to someone else," he said softly when he came back to Bethany's end of the bar.

"Oh no!" Her heart went out to Maggie.

A moment later, Maggie returned to the bar, with a smile on her face, until Ryder pulled her aside and warned her. Her face turned ashen. He said something else, and she nodded. But first she walked over to Jason and his fiancé.

"Hello Jason. It's nice to see you. My shift is just ending, but I wanted to say hi first. I see congratulations are in order."

Jason at least looked somewhat uncomfortable. "Hi Maggie, I didn't even think that you might be on the bar. We're meeting some friends and got here a little early. This is Tiffany. She works with me at the bank."

"It's nice to meet you." Tiffany's voice was high pitched and annoying.

"Well, enjoy your evening." Maggie turned and left and when she glanced over at Ryder and Bethany, she looked on the verge of tears. She nodded at both of them and grabbed her purse from under the bar.

"Thanks, Ryder. I owe you."

She disappeared into the kitchen which led out to the back parking lot as Ryder let out a heavy sigh. "I told her to just go, that I'd cover the rest of her shift tonight. Poor kid."

"Is she still hung up on him?" Bethany asked.

"No, I really don't think she is. But I knew the shock of seeing him here with his new finance would be too much for her. She doesn't need to wait on them. Not while I'm here."

She smiled. He was a great big brother.

"She's lucky to have you."

He shook his head and reached for his beer. "I'd do the same for anyone in these circumstances." He turned as a crowd of guys came in and lined up at the bar. Bethany took her last sip of wine and put it in the bar dishwasher.

"I'm going to head out. I'll see you tomorrow."

CHAPTER 12

"You're flying out to New York tomorrow morning and coming back the next day? Are you sure you want to do that?" Bethany's mother looked at her as though she'd lost her marbles.

"I'm sure. I've had all week to think about it and I think it's a sign. It's time to put the condo on the market. And I need to get it ready to be shown and meet with the realtor." Gina Corcoran had texted her earlier in the week and asked if she might be ready to list her unit as they had several buyers interested in her building.

The market was hot, and she didn't expect that it would take long to sell if it was priced right. It was Bethany's last connection to Manhattan, but it was silly to keep paying the mortgage every month if she wasn't living there and if she had no intention of moving back.

"It's a good time to sell." She got all the ingredients for her mother's favorite lemongrass smoothie and made one for both of them. She brought the smoothies and a cup of black coffee to the kitchen table where her mother was reading the paper.

"Thanks, honey." Her mother stuck a straw in the smoothie and took a sip. Bethany noticed that her hair was growing in nicely now and was a little curly. That was new though they said it often happened to people who had chemotherapy. Overall, her mother looked and felt really good. And her doctor was encouraged by her progress.

"How are you feeling?" she asked.

"I'm great. Marcia's going to stop by later this morning and we're going walking and then out to lunch with Glenda and Janie."

"That sounds fun."

After she finished her smoothie and cleaned up the kitchen, Bethany took her last sip of coffee and headed to the restaurant.

All the Quinn's were there when she arrived and it looked like they were having some kind of family meeting. Ryder looked up when Bethany walked in. She didn't want to interrupt and was going to keep walking to the kitchen but Ryder called her over.

"Let's ask Bethany's opinion."

She smiled. "My opinion for what?"

"Once a month, the whole family gets together for

dinner. Just the family. It's this Sunday night, and she wants to invite Harry Peterman. It just doesn't seem appropriate. What do you think?"

"Oh, um. Well. Who is hosting?" she finally managed.

"My mother always hosts," Maggie said. Her eyes were stormy and it was clear how she felt about the matter.

"Well, if your mother is hosting, then I think it's her decision who to invite."

"Thanks, Bethany. I quite agree." His mother looked pleased.

Ryder sighed. "You're no help at all."

She laughed. "Sorry about that."

A mischievous gleam came into his mother's eyes. "Would it make you feel better if I told you to invite Bethany? I'm sure she'd enjoy having dinner with us."

Family dinner with the Quinn's. Bethany didn't know what to think.

"What do you say, Bethany? Want to join this crazy bunch for dinner?" Ryder asked.

She did actually. In the past two weeks, she and Ryder had been spending a lot of time together. Just about every night they had a drink or two after work. They hadn't gone on an actual date yet, but Bethany was comfortable with how things were progressing and she imagined that Ryder was being cautious since she worked for him too. But, she definitely sensed the interest. She could see it in his eyes. She was happy just spending time with him. And she felt bad that she had to decline their invitation.

"I'd love to, but I can't this Sunday night. I'm flying to New York in the morning and meeting with a realtor. I'm putting my condo on the market."

"Oh. Okay. Well, that's good then. When do you come back?"

"Monday, late afternoon."

"That's a fast trip," Maggie commented.

"I know. It's not ideal, but I didn't want to miss work."

"You can't do it over the phone?" his mother asked.

"No, not really. I need to declutter my condo a little and get it ready to show well."

She didn't mention that she was also going to meet with her former boss, Mark Newton. He said he wanted to show her the new restaurant he was going to be opening. He also said he wanted her to come with him as his executive chef and the salary he mentioned was dizzying.

But it was an easy decision to say no. It wasn't what she wanted to do or where she wanted to be anymore. And she told him as much, but he still insisted that she come see the restaurant and have a drink with him 'for old times sake.' She knew Mark well enough to know that he was going to try to put the pressure on to change her mind, but she didn't mind meeting him for one drink. She owed him a lot, and she was curious to see what his new venture was going to be like.

She had one drink at the bar with Ryder and Maggie at the end of the night. They were both in great moods as it had been a busy night and in the past two weeks, sales had gone up significantly and word was getting around about the new menu. They had a steady stream of tourists coming in too using the discount coupons. And Bethany was thrilled to see that they were now rated the top restaurant in Quinn Valley on TripAdvisor.

She smiled as she saw two couples at the bar drinking coffee and sharing a piece of chocolate cake. As she'd hoped, it had become a popular favorite and was mentioned in most of their rave reviews. One of the reviews even said that after eating the chocolate cake, a woman's boyfriend went out the very next day and bought an engagement ring. Stories like that warmed Bethany's heart.

"So, I'm finally going to meet my mystery man with the great voice," Maggie said.

"Charlie Harris?" Ryder asked.

She nodded. "He told me yesterday that Sean, the regular salesman, is going on vacation in April. And he'll be covering then and making the deliveries."

Bethany laughed. "In April? That's like six months or so from now. That's funny"

"I know, right? It's all just teasing fun. I do look forward to talking to him though. I have to admit I'm curious to see what he looks like."

"You need to go on a date before then," Ryder said.

Maggie surprised them both by agreeing. "I know. And I have one lined up for next Thursday night. A friend of Sally's new boyfriend. We're going to see a concert in Lewiston."

"That sounds fun." Bethany was glad that Maggie was going to put herself out there. A new customer came to the bar, and she went to take his order.

Ryder looked thoughtful as he took a sip his beer. He set the glass down and turned to her. "What do you say we go on a real date when you get back? Like out to dinner. Wherever you want to go?"

"Oh. I'd love that. It would be nice to see some of the other local restaurants. I really haven't been anywhere since I got home, except for here and O'Shea's."

"There's a few good places in town and in Riston there's an Italian restaurant that I love. They have good cannoli."

"That sounds perfect." Bethany yawned as she checked the time on her cell phone. It was getting late, and she had to be up really early. She pushed her half full glass of wine away and fished in her purse for some cash.

"You didn't even finish your wine. Your half-glass is on me. Have a safe trip, Bethany."

CHAPTER 13

Bethany drove to the Lewiston airport at the obscene hour of three am to get there an hour ahead of her five am flight. There were no good options for flying to New York City from Lewiston. There were no direct flights and even leaving this early didn't get her there until after three in the afternoon because of the time difference. But it would work out because she was meeting Mark later that evening, and the realtor was coming first thing in the morning.

She took an Uber from the airport to her tiny condo. It had one small bedroom that barely fit her bed, a gallery kitchen and a small sitting area. It was in an up-and-coming area of the city though and had a small balcony where she used to love to sit and have her morning coffee when it was nice out. She looked around the small space which felt even smaller after coming from her mother's house, which wasn't big but was a lot more spacious than this. Bethany remembered when she'd first moved in and was so excited about buying her first home.

But with what she'd get for it, she could buy a house three times the size or more in Quinn Valley. She didn't have any plans to buy anything anytime soon, but it would be nice to not have to worry about making the monthly payments anymore and to have a nest egg in the bank.

She spent the rest of the afternoon straightening up and throwing things out that were just taking up space. By the time she finished, she had about an hour to get ready and meet Mark at the address he'd given her. A hot shower felt great and a half hour later, she was dressed and in an Uber on her way to Mark's new restaurant.

The address was a trendy brownstone in mid-town Manhattan and Mark was sitting on the front step checking something on his phone when she stepped out of the car. He looked up when he heard her footsteps and pulled her in for a hug.

"Thanks for coming. You look amazing as always." Mark always was a flatterer. But Bethany did feel good. She hadn't had a reason to get dressed up since she'd been back in Quinn Valley and the black dress she wore was one of her favorites. It was modestly cut and flattering.

"You look great too. Your hair looks different. Did you color it?" His hair was thick and choppy and she was pretty sure it was also blonder than she'd last seen it.

He laughed. "Ssssh, don't tell anyone. I'm going for the hot, surfer look. What do you think?"

She just shook her head. "I think you haven't changed at all!"

"Ha! Come on inside. I want to show you what I'm planning."

She followed him inside and gasped when he turned the lights on. The space was absolutely gorgeous. Huge bay windows looked out over a court-yard that was draped in tiny white lights. All the tables were covered in a shimmery blue gray fabric and accented with creamy white napkins. Black vases filled with white flowers sat in the middle of every table. The overall look was both elegant and warm.

"It's beautiful. What's the menu like?"

"That's the best part. It's right up your alley. I'm thinking upscale comfort food. That's why I thought of you first."

The space and overall concept would have been her dream situation if she wanted to stay in the city.

"It's tempting. I can't say it's not. But I'm selling my condo and staying in Idaho. It's time."

Mark looked at her as if she had two heads. "How can you say no to this? To living here? There's no greater city on earth."

Bethany laughed. "I agree. But I don't want to live in any city anymore."

Mark sighed. "Okay, I'll give up, for now. Let's have a glass of wine and then grab a bite to eat. There's a new place that opened up in Soho that I've been meaning to check out. You okay with red?" He began rummaging through a wine closet until he found what he was looking for.

"Red is fine."

"Good. Because this one is going to knock your socks off."

~

BETHANY HAD A BIT OF A HEADACHE THE NEXT morning when the realtor knocked at the door. She was glad that she'd taken the time the day before to straighten up so the place looked neat and ready to show. Gina bounced through the door and was so perky and chipper that Bethany wanted to groan.

"Would you like some coffee?" she offered.

"Oh no, I'm fine. I already had mine at the office."

Bethany topped off her mug and walked around the condo with Gina while she asked questions and took notes.

"This is such a great neighborhood. Will you be looking to buy something else in the city?"

"No. I don't think so. I've loved living here though." It was going to be bittersweet to leave.

"So, I think I can get this sold for you quickly, if you're ready to get started?"

"I'm as ready as I'll ever be." They discussed a starting price, and Bethany signed the necessary paperwork. She gave Gina a spare set of keys and told her she could show the condo anytime as she wouldn't be there.

"Okay, stay tuned. I'll be in touch!" When Gina left all the energy went out of the room and Bethany sank into a chair at her small kitchen table. She sipped her coffee and slowly felt her headache ebb away. She and Mark had stayed up late, drinking wine and eating so many wonderful things. He insisted on getting the tasting menu and knew the chef, so there was much discussion about the different dishes and cooking in general.

It was the kind of night that Bethany loved. She could talk about food until the wee hours. And they did. It was after one by the time Mark dropped her at her building. Several times throughout the night he'd asked her again if she'd reconsider but she told him no every time.

"You're a tough nut to crack," he said when he stopped outside her building. "If you change your mind, call me. I'm looking to nail down my chef in the next few weeks."

"Thank you for a wonderful night, Mark. It was great to see you again. And I wish you all the best with the new restaurant."

"Safe travels, Bethany."

CHAPTER 14

Ryder was earlier than usual Tuesday morning. He'd been antsy since Sunday when Bethany left for New York. He knew she was going there to list her condo, which he thoroughly approved of but a small part of him still worried that she might change her mind and decide to move back there. What if she realized how much she missed the city?

He wanted to believe her though when she said she was back in Quinn Valley for good. Until he'd walked in that morning and his mother announced that she was his new chef, he'd pretty much given up on the possibility. And he'd tried to move on. He really had. But there was only one Bethany.

And unless he imagined it, she was feeling some of the same things he was. He loved everything about her, her laugh, her shy smile, her amazing cooking, her sense of humor, the way she laughed at his lame attempts at a joke and the way she looked. She took his breath away, she always had. There was no one else he'd rather spend time with and he'd been surprised by how much he'd missed not seeing her for the past few days.

He'd quickly grown so used to seeing her every day, and looked forward to sharing a drink after work and chatting about all the crazy things that had happened that day. Yes, it was definitely time for he and Bethany to officially start dating.

"Morning." The familiar voice made him feel warm inside. He turned and saw Bethany standing in a pool of light that streamed through the open window. She was wearing faded jeans, her hair was in a ponytail and she was carrying a hot coffee. And she'd never looked so beautiful. He fought the urge to go and kiss her senseless. He knew that wouldn't be appropriate. Instead he smiled and asked how her trip was.

"It was fine and fast. I'm tired today as you can imagine, but I got the condo listed and my realtor thinks it should go quickly. There's not much available in my price range."

"So, you're back to stay awhile," he teased.

She hesitated for a second and then smiled. "Of course I'm here to stay. How was your family dinner? Did Mr. Peterman go?"

"He did. He seems to go everywhere with my mother now. She keeps insisting though that they are just good friends."

Bethany laughed. "Well, it sounds like they really are good friends."

"Right. Oh, I had a message that my grandmother and her friends are coming today for a late lunch. And she has a special request."

"Oh? What's that?"

"Apparently they all want that lemongrass smoothie that you made for your mother. Word has gotten around that it's some kind of cure all. My grandmother also wants you to set aside three pieces of chocolate cake for the table to share."

"Is that all they want? Smoothies and chocolate cake?" Bethany was amused.

"I don't ask questions. I just do what she says," Ryder said.

∾

LATER THAT AFTERNOON, RYDER CAME INTO THE kitchen and looked a bit uncomfortable.

"My grandmother wants to talk to you. If it's not too much trouble. Her words."

She laughed. "I'd be happy to talk to her. Where is she?"

"Round table by the window, white hair, purple sweater and pearls."

Bethany ducked into the bathroom to smooth her hair, added a bit of lipstick to freshen her look and made her way into the dining room. She immediately recognized Ryder's grandmother. She was sitting in the middle of the table, and the surrounding ladies were hanging on her every word. She finished her story just as Bethany reached the table and the ladies broke into peals of laughter.

"Well, hello there. It's been a long time since I've seen you Bethany. It's very kind of you to come see us."

"I hope that you enjoyed your lunch? Ryder said that you wanted to talk to me?"

"Yes. Tell me dear, how is your mother? Is she doing better? I heard that she's been ill."

Bethany smiled. "She's doing very well. Her doctor says her tests are all showing significant improvement."

"Oh, that is wonderful news." All the ladies nodded in agreement.

"That smoothie we had, with the lemongrass, is that what your mother drank?"

"Yes, she still has one every day."

"You don't say. And will these be available here regularly now?"

"The smoothies? I think so yes."

"Good, because we're all hoping that they might help us too. None of us are as sick as your poor mother of course, but we figure it might be good to keep ahead of things. Build up our immune system."

Bethany was impressed. "I really do think it helps."

"And what about the chocolate cake?" His grandmother winked. "Do you suppose that helps too?"

Bethany grinned "I know that it helps. It feeds the soul."

"That it does. So, my grandson. Are the two of you dating yet?"

"Gertrude!" Her friend Nellie nudged her.

"It's an honest question. Inquiring minds would like to know." The ladies all leaned forward in their chairs, listening hard.

"Ryder and I are very good friends," Bethany said.

"Hmmmm. Well, I suppose that will have to do for now. Thanks for coming to see us." Bethany fought back the urge to giggle. She was being dismissed.

"Enjoy the rest of your day, ladies."

∾

SHE STOPPED BY THE BAR TO GET A GLASS OF WATER on her way back to the kitchen. Maggie was unloading the dishwasher and looked up when she saw her.

"Was my grandmother giving you the third-degree? She prides herself on her matchmaking abilities."

Bethany chuckled. "Not too bad. She was equally interested in making sure the lemongrass smoothie stays on the menu."

"Now she's into smoothies? She's too much."

"I hope I have half her energy when I get to be her age."

"She does pretty well. She doesn't miss much that's for sure. Grandma seems to know about everything that goes on around here."

"I heard Mr. Peterman came to dinner. How was it?" Bethany asked.

"Not as bad as I thought it might be. He's actually a pretty nice guy. And he's obviously crazy about my mother, so I have to like that about him."

"Ryder says that she says they are just friends."

"That's right. Very good friends. I don't think she's looking to rush anything, which is smart of her. Oh, gotta go. New people needing drinks."

Bethany made her way back to the kitchen and got ready for the dinner rush. When it quieted down, a few hours later, she joined her mother and her friends. Jill was delivering a baby so she couldn't make it. But Ryder joined them too.

"I hear you put your Manhattan condo on the market?" Glenda asked as Ivy set down Bethany's wine and Ryder's beer.

"I did, yes." Bethany's phone beeped alerting her that she had a text message. It was from Gina. She read the message and smiled.

"That was just my realtor, letting me know that she has two showings scheduled for this week."

"That was fast," her mother said.

"She said the market is hot. We'll see what happens."

"Well, cheers to a quick sale." Ryder lifted his beer glass and the others all did the same.

"So, I had an interesting phone call a few minutes ago too. Gary and Suzanne were arrested in Las Vegas for running a similar scam on the restaurant they were working at."

"Wow, they caught them pretty quickly," Bethany said.

"In Vegas they have cameras everywhere because of the casinos. It wasn't very smart of them." He explained to her mother's friends what they'd done at Quinn's.

"How awful," Janie said. "Will they go to jail now?"

"It looks like they will. They won't be able to rip anyone else off for a long time now."

"Are you all playing music bingo tonight?" Eddie, the game's host was handing out score sheets and pads of paper for their answers.

"We're in," Ryder said.

Two hours later, they officially came in last place after blowing the final question.

"Oh well, you win some, you lose some," her mother said.

"That's right, but it's always fun," Glenda agreed.

They settled their bill and everyone left together. Ryder and Bethany walked her mother to her car and then as soon as she drove off, Ryder pulled Bethany to him and brought his lips to hers. He took her by surprise but his kiss was welcome and just as sweet as she remembered.

"I've been waiting a long time to do that. I've missed kissing you." he said.

"I've missed it too."

"Are you ready for that real date we talked about? We could go Sunday night if you're interested?"

"I'm interested."

He took her hand and walked her to her car and kissed her again. This time the kiss went on forever, but it was still too short for Bethany's liking. Ryder gave a final hug before she got into her car.

"Sleep tight, Bethany."

CHAPTER 15

The rest of the week flew by in a happy blur. Every night after work, she sat with Ryder and Maggie and then Ryder walked her to her car and they kissed, for a long time. On Sunday were going to his favorite Italian restaurant in Riston, the next town over and she was looking forward to it. Though she didn't really care where they went as long as they were together.

And when Sunday morning came, she and her mother went to the spa at the Quinn hotel for massages and then a long hot soak in the hot springs. They'd both been before of course, because how could you live in Quinn Valley and never visit the hot springs? But it had been many years since either of them had been. She knew it was supposed to have healing properties too.

"How does it feel?" she asked her mother as they relaxed in the warm water.

"Heavenly. It's like nature's hot tub."

Bethany smiled. "We really should do this more often."

Once they were done soaking and got dressed, they took a drive downtown and had a nice lunch at Phil's diner. She'd been going there with her mother for as long as she could remember. And they almost always got the same thing. Chocolate shakes, cheese burgers and onion rings.

"I love all that healthy food you've had me eating, but sometimes a little grease is good." Her mother winked as she took a big bite of her burger. A minute later she asked, "So, Ryder's taking you out to dinner tonight. Will this be your first real date?"

"It will. In a way though, because I see him every day and night, it almost feels like we've been together longer."

"Well, you do have some history."

"That's true. Though it feels like it was a million years ago."

"You're still the same people. Just older, and hopefully wiser." Her mother reached for an onion ring and dunked it in ketchup before taking a bite.

"I hope we're wiser. We'll find out I guess."

Her mother frowned. "Well that doesn't sound very optimistic. I think the two of you belong together. I always have. Don't worry so much. Just enjoy every day as it comes. That's something I've learned recently."

"You're right." Bethany took a sip of her chocolate

shake. It was rich and creamy and probably not at all what she should be having since she was going out to dinner later. "Your pet scan is tomorrow right? I can go with you if you like?" She knew her mother was nervous about what the results of the full body scan would be.

"I'd like that. I've been falling asleep with my crystals every night....I'm feeling hopeful."

"I am too."

BETHANY TRIED ON AT LEAST A DOZEN OUTFITS before finally settling on her favorite faded jeans, a white top with a long, flowing caramel cashmere sweater over it and black leather cowboy boots. She ran a curling iron through her hair to add some soft, tousled waves and finished the look with a deep rose lipstick. She almost felt like she was back in high school as she waited for her date to come and pick her up. When she heard the knock at the door, the butterflies in her stomach went crazy. She told herself it was silly. It was just Ryder after all and she'd known him forever.

But when she came downstairs and saw him chatting with her mother, she just stared for a minute. She hadn't seen Ryder all dressed up in a long time. He was looking sharp in a button-down shirt and tie and a navy blazer over jeans. His hair was lightly gelled and when he turned her way and smiled, his cute dimple and his eyes fought for her attention. The eyes won as they always did.

"Hi, Ryder."

"Bethany. You look beautiful."

"She does, doesn't she?" her mother said proudly.

"Thank you. See you in a while, mom."

"You two have fun."

Bethany stepped outside and saw Ryder's car at the curb. They drove off and spent the whole ride laughing about silly things they'd seen that week at the restaurant. There was no shortage of stories to share. The ride to Riston went by in no time and they soon arrived at Mamma Mia's, the Italian restaurant Ryder liked so much.

She was glad to see that they were busy, but not too busy. There were a few empty tables, and they were led to a nice one by a cozy fireplace.

Their server appeared a minute or so later to take their drink order and they ordered a bottle of chianti.

Once the wine was poured, and they put their orders in, Ryder picked up his glass and tapped it against hers.

"To our first real date. First of many I hope."

Bethany looked around the room, at the cheerful glow of the fire, the hum of conversation around them and the smell of garlic and tomatoes. Their server returned to their table and set down a basket of hot crusty bread and a dish of olive oil and spices.

"I can see why you like it here," she said as she took

a piece of bread and dunked it in the fragrant oil. And then she shared her big news.

"So, I got a call from my realtor today. She had two showings this week on my condo. And both people made an offer."

"Wow! That's good news. The market must really be hot there."

"That's what she said, but I didn't realize it would happen that quickly."

Ryder frowned. "Are you sure you want to sell?"

"Oh, I'm sure. I accepted one of the offers. We close in a month."

"That's great! Congratulations." He was quiet for a moment and then said, "Did I tell you I'm thinking about building a house?"

"No. What kind of house? Where?"

"I bought a lot of land a few years ago as an investment. It's on a lake and is a good size, over two acres. I thought at one point that I might want to subdivide and sell it, but it's a really pretty spot and I think I want to keep it as is."

"I've always thought it would be fun to build my own dream house. To get everything exactly the way I want it."

"What would that look like to you?" Ryder broke off a piece of bread and dipped it in the oil.

Bethany thought about that for a minute. "Maybe a rustic contemporary style with lots of big windows that would overlook the water, and a big deck to sit outside and have coffee."

"That sounds good. What else?"

"Three or maybe four bedrooms in case I have children at some point. A comfortable living room or family room and of course an amazing kitchen."

"Of course."

"What would you want?" she asked.

"Not too different. Most of what you said, plus a basement for a man cave and a three-car garage."

"But you only have one car."

"For now. I might want more and maybe I might live with someone someday and that person probably would have a car."

"True. Where do you live now?" The last time they dated, Ryder lived at home with his family.

"I'm renting for now, a condo not far from the restaurant. It's convenient but kind of vanilla. I'm looking forward to having a little more space. And the lake lot isn't far, maybe a ten minute drive to Quinn's."

THEIR MEALS WERE DELIVERED A FEW MINUTES later, chicken parmesan for Ryder and gnocchi with meatballs for Bethany. The potato based pasta was homemade and cooked to perfection, light and pillowy and the sauce was delicious. Ryder looked happy with his dinner too. As they ate and chatted, Bethany noticed the way Ryder's dimple and the laugh lines around his mouth and eyes made his face so attractive.

He seemed more relaxed now than when she first

started at the restaurant too. There was a nervous tension around him then that she knew was partly due to her sudden appearance but also his worries about the restaurants financial situation. She was relieved that sales were still trending upwards and that feedback so far on the food had been overwhelmingly positive.

"I had an interesting phone call before I left to pick you up," Ryder began.

"Oh?"

"A buddy of mine works at the newspaper and told me to be sure to check the review page tomorrow. Evidently their lifestyles editor that also does the occasional restaurant review was in last week sometime for dinner."

Bethany felt a pit in her stomach. She'd seen the damage a bad review could do to a restaurant before.

"Was he warning you? Or do you think it might be positive?"

"He didn't say, probably couldn't say until the review is live. But, he was in a good mood. And I can't imagine anyone would give your food a bad review."

"Well, I hope he liked whatever he had. A good review could be helpful."

"Don't be all worried now. I really do think this is probably good news. Let's toast to the possibility of it." He raised his glass and Bethany laughed and tapped hers against his and took a sip.

"Now, let's just hope you didn't jinx us!"

He chuckled. "I don't believe in jinxing. But I do

believe in you. I wouldn't say this in front of my mother, but you're a better chef than she is."

"Thank you. And no, that can never be said to her! Besides, I had the advantage of formal training."

Ryder took his last bite of chicken and set his fork down. He'd cleaned his plate while Bethany still had more than half of her dinner left. She'd be taking the rest home with her.

"Did you save any room for dessert?" he asked.

"I'm pretty stuffed. But if you want something, I could probably take a bite or two to help."

He grinned. "Let's share a cannoli. "

Their server cleared their plates and set a single cannoli between them along with two forks. It was one of Bethany's favorite desserts and this one looked just like the ones she used to get in New York's Little Italy restaurants. The ricotta filling was rich and creamy with a hint of sweetness and the edges were dipped in tiny chocolate chips. The shell was crisp and the perfect vehicle for the filling. She had two small bites and let Ryder finish the rest.

"Good, huh?" he said as he polished off the last bite..

"So good."

Ryder reached for the bill when it was delivered and handed it back to the server with his credit card.

"Where should we go from here? Figs on Main Street usually has live music if you want to check that out. It's not too far of a walk from here."

"Sure. I could use a good walk."

After Ryder signed the credit card slip, Bethany put her bag with her leftovers in the car and they walked over to Figs. The air was brisk and cool with a slight wind as they walked. Bethany snuggled into her coat to ward off the wind and was glad when they reached Figs a few minutes later. The restaurant bar was warm and lively as they stepped inside. It looked like a small band was getting ready to play a set.

There were no open cocktail tables or seats at the bar, but there was a spot against the wall where they could be out of the way and also have a good view of the music.

"What can I get you? I'm going to go up to the bar."

"I'd love a coffee, with a little Frangelico in it."

Ryder smiled. "And whipped cream?"

"Of course!"

While he was getting their drinks at the bar, Bethany watched the band get ready. There were two guys on guitar and a pretty woman with long caramel colored wavy hair. She looked vaguely familiar and Bethany wondered if she might have seen her somewhere before.

She noticed Ryder chatting with a guy at the bar. It looked like they knew each other. He returned with their drinks a few minutes later and handed Bethany her coffee. She took a sip. The hot coffee and nutty flavor of the hazelnut liqueur warmed her right up.

"What are you drinking?" Ryder was sipping something clear with a lemon floating in it.

"Just soda water. I'm too full for anything else and still have to drive us back."

"True. Who was that you were talking to at the bar?"

"That's Wade. Wade Weston. He's the general manager of the River's End Ranch resort here in Riston. I know him from college. He's a great guy. He said that Lily, the singer in the band tonight, also works for him handling events."

"Oh, I thought she looked familiar! I think my mother mentioned something about her a while back. There was an article about her in the local paper. She's a songwriter too, right?"

"I think so. Oh, and I talked to Wade briefly about our discount coupons. He thought that was a great idea and said he might want to have some to give out at the ranch too."

"Don't they have a restaurant at the ranch too?"

"Yes, but he knows the guests won't want to go there every night. And the hot springs in Quinn Valley is a perfect day trip for people staying at River's End. And if they come to our town, we're happy to feed them."

When the band began to play, Ryder put his arms around her and she leaned into him, listening and enjoying the music. So far, it had been a perfect night and being in Ryder's arms was exactly where she wanted to be. She sighed with happiness.

"Having fun?" he whispered in her ear.

"Yes. So much fun."

They left after the band finished their set. The temperature had dropped even more and the walk back to the car was a cold one. Ryder turned on the heat as soon as they drove out of town and it didn't take long to warm up. Bethany wasn't eager for the evening to end, but it wasn't long before Ryder pulled onto her mother's street and stopped in front of her house. He jumped out of the car and came around to open her door, which made her smile. He was such a gentleman.

"Don't forget tomorrow's lunch." He handed her the small bag that was on the floor of the car.

"Thank you. And thank you for a wonderful night."

"It's not over just yet. I still need to kiss you." He pulled her close and brought his lips to hers. She inhaled his scent, the fresh wonderful smell that was uniquely his. It was addicting, and she leaned into him and deepened the kiss. If it wasn't so cold, she could have kissed him much longer, but when she shivered, he pulled back.

"I think that's our sign to call it a night."

"I suppose you're right."

"And you have a big day tomorrow. Big for your mom that is." She'd told him about the scan her mother was going for and how they were hoping for good news.

"Yes. We're all praying hard."

"Well, let her know she's in my thoughts and my mother's too. And Maggie's."

"I will. Goodnight, Ryder."

CHAPTER 16

When Bethany came downstairs the next morning, her mother was already in the kitchen making herself a smoothie.

"Morning. Do you want me to do that?" Her mother had all the ingredients lined up on the counter and was staring at the juicer.

"If you could just show me how to work this thing, I'm happy to do it. That way I can make these anytime."

Bethany showed her how to feed the fruit and vegetables into the juicing machine and the best way to clean it immediately afterward so it didn't get all sticky.

She poured herself a coffee while her mother sipped her smoothie. They had to leave for the hospital shortly.

"So, did you have fun last night? I went to bed early and never heard you come in."

"We did have fun. We went to Figs after dinner to hear some music."

"Figs. I think I went there a few years ago, right on Main street?"

"That's the place. We didn't eat there, but the menu looked good. The food at Mamma Mia's was excellent."

Her mother nodded. "It's been a long time since I've been there, but I remember it always being very good."

Her mother looked serious and hopeful as she leaned forward and said, "So, what do you think about Ryder? Are the two of you an item now?"

"Yes. I think so. I know that's what I want."

Her mother smiled. "Good."

They spent the rest of the day at the hospital and Bethany spent most of her time waiting, while her mother got ready to have her Pet Scan, which involved injecting a dye that would allow the machines to scan her whole body and determine if there was any cancer left and where it was. The procedure itself took awhile and then the recovery period. Once she was done, they went straight home and Bethany served her mother a big bowl of chicken soup and some hot bread. She was starving because she wasn't able to eat solid foods before the test. The test results would take two business days her doctor told them, so they spent the next two days worrying and waiting. And on Thursday morning, a few minutes before Bethany left to go to work, her mother's doctor called.

She was silent on the phone, just listening as he told her the results of the scan. And she looked to be in a bit of a daze as she thanked him for calling and hung up the phone. She burst into tears which alarmed Bethany until she saw her smile emerge.

"He said that there was nothing on the scans. No signs of any cancer at all."

And suddenly Bethany was crying too and hugging her mother.

"I'm so happy for you, Mom."

"And I'm so grateful, honey. Everything you've done, the smoothies, crystals, oils, and the hot springs. I think it all helped so much."

"I don't know what worked, I'm just glad we tried everything, and the something did the trick."

"Marcia is coming by for tea today. I think we may need to go out to lunch and celebrate instead."

"Why don't you come into Quinn's? Maggie and Ryder are going to be so excited for you too."

"Maybe we will!"

RYDER WAS IN A BETTER THAN USUAL MOOD WHEN he arrived at Quinn's Thursday morning. His night with Bethany had gone even better than he'd hoped and they'd spent the next few evenings together too. He could finally see himself building a future with her. It also made him feel more secure that she'd already sold her Manhattan condo, so in a month, when she closed on the sale, she wouldn't have any more ties there.

Maggie was already there, sitting at the bar going over her weekly order. She was on her phone and finished her call as he brought his coffee over to the bar and sat next to her. He noticed that she was blushing slightly and seemed a bit flustered, which was unlike her.

He smiled. "Have you been talking to Charlie again?"

Her flush deepened and she nodded. "I'm almost afraid to meet him. We have such a perfect relationship over the phone. He flirts with me and makes me laugh. And that voice."

"You have it bad."

She sighed. "I think it's a fantasy, really. It's not real."

"You never know. Stranger things have happened. You should meet him."

"I will. But not until April."

He laughed. "Whatever makes you happy."

Bethany came through the door and rushed over to them. She looked happier than he'd ever seen her.

"You look like you won the lottery!" Maggie said.

"Better. My mother got her scan results this morning and there's no trace left of her cancer."

Maggie came out from behind the bar, her eyes suddenly wet and pulled Bethany in for a hug. "That's the best news ever."

And Bethany's eyes were shiny too as she smiled

up at him. There was so much love there, and he was happy for both of them.

He pulled her in for a hug too and kissed her forehead gently. "Please tell your mother we're both thrilled for her."

She grinned. "You can tell her yourself! I think your mother and my mother are coming in for lunch today to celebrate."

"Oh great. I'll reserve our best table by the window for them."

"Thanks. She'd love that."

Maggie went back to her ordering and Ryder walked with Bethany into the kitchen. They chatted about her next order from David. She wanted to try some of the products they'd tasted.

"Go ahead, I trust you completely on the menu. You haven't steered us wrong yet."

"Thank you. Oh, and I know I said it last night, but I had a really good time with you. It was the perfect date."

He smiled. He couldn't seem to stop smiling around Bethany lately. She had that effect on him.

"Let's do it again this Sunday. I'm not much of a cook, but I can grill a steak and I want to show you my lot by the lake. We can take a drive out there if you like?"

"I'd love to see it, and I'm always up for a good steak."

"Great, it's a date then."

~

BETHANY WAS HAVING A GREAT DAY. SHE COULDN'T remember when she'd last felt so happy. Her mother was healthy and she was looking forward to spending her day off with Ryder. She stayed busy in the kitchen through the lunch rush and then took a break to visit with her mother and Marcia. They'd come in for a late lunch when they knew it wouldn't be too busy so everyone could stop by their table and celebrate the good news.

After they left, Bethany was on her way back into the kitchen when a familiar face walked into the bar. Mark Newton. He looked around as if he was searching for someone and broke into a huge grin when he saw her.

"I was hoping I'd come to the right place!"

She walked over to him. He went to give her a hug, and she took a step back. Ryder and Maggie were watching with interest at the bar and she didn't want there to be any misunderstandings. Mark had no business being in Quinn Valley and at her restaurant as far as she knew. Which meant he'd come for one reason, to see her.

"What are you doing here?"

"Can we meet for a drink after you finish up?"

She knew that wouldn't go over well with Ryder and she couldn't blame him. Plus she had no interest in meeting Mark for another drink. "No, I'm working late tonight. What is it?"

He glanced around the bar and his gaze stopped for a minute on Ryder and Maggie.

"Is that your boss? The glaring man at the end of the bar?"

"Yes, he and his sister own Quinn's."

"Okay. Well maybe we should step outside for a minute. This won't take long."

"I've got about two minutes to spare."

"I'll make it fast."

She followed him outside and crossed her arms over her chest waiting for him to say what he came to say.

"Why did you fly all the way here? You could have just called me or texted."

"I did both, but I didn't hear back from you."

Hmmmm Maybe he did, she hadn't checked her text messages in a few days and she had ignored his last voice message.

"Here's the thing. I really want you to be my executive chef."

Bethany sighed. "We already had this conversation."

"No, I know. Hear me out. So, I've been thinking and I have the perfect solution. I'll cut you in, make you a partner. You'll get a share of all the profits. So you'll have a little skin in the game. What do you say? It's an opportunity you can't pass up right?"

She looked at him. A few months ago he would have been right. It was the kind of opportunity she'd dreamed of. But her dreams had changed. And Mark wasn't in them.

"I'm hugely flattered, but no thank you. This is where I want to be. Where I need to be."

Mark didn't look happy. He tried one last time."But this isn't Manhattan."

She smiled. "No, it's not. It's home. Goodbye, Mark."

BETHANY WENT BACK INSIDE AND WALKED OVER TO Ryder and Maggie.

"Who was that?" Maggie asked. Ryder said nothing, just waited for her to explain.

"That's Mark Newton. I used to work for him."

"And he just happened to drop by Quinn Valley?" Ryder raised his eyebrows. The wariness she'd seen in his eyes when she first saw him, was back.

"I saw him in Manhattan too when I went home to put the condo on the market. He wanted to meet me for a drink and to show me his new restaurant."

"He offered you a job." Ryder's tone was flat and cold.

She nodded. "He did. But I turned him down."

"Why did you even meet with him if you weren't considering it?" he asked

"I knew I didn't want it. But I felt I owed it to him to take the meeting, and I was curious to see what he was doing," she admitted.

"If you said no, why did he come here?" Maggie looked confused.

"Mark never was good at taking no for an answer. He raised the stakes and offered me shares in the restaurant."

"So you'd be an owner. I'd imagine that's hard to say no to," Maggie said.

"A few months ago it would have been." She looked at Ryder and smiled. "But today it was easy."

"You told him to beat it?" He sounded surprised, and unsure if he believed her.

"I did. I told you the other night that I sold my condo."

"You don't close for a month. You could still get out of it," he said.

"I probably could. But I don't want to. I'm happy here. I don't want to go back to Manhattan. Except maybe for a vacation."

Ryder smiled tightly. "I can think of a long list of other places I'd rather go on vacation."

Maggie laughed and went off to help a new customer.

"So, are we good? Still on for Sunday?" Bethany asked. Ryder still seemed a little distant and closed off.

"Sure. We're still on for Sunday."

RYDER WATCHED HER GO BACK TO THE KITCHEN and stewed for a minute longer before heading into his office. He'd been looking forward to Sunday and was eager to show Bethany his land and to cook for her. He needed to digest everything that he'd just heard though and make sure that they were both on the same page. Maybe Bethany wasn't as far along as he was with where he thought their relationship was going.

CHAPTER 17

Ryder was quiet the rest of the day on Thursday which concerned Bethany a bit, but he still wanted her to stay after work that night and they kept Maggie company at the bar for about an hour or so before calling it a night. And he still walked her to her car and gave her a kiss goodnight. It wasn't as long or as passionate as the one she'd had the night before, but it was still a pretty good kiss as far as kisses went.

By Saturday, things seemed back to normal with them and Bethany relaxed fully. Her heart had sank when she saw Mark walk into Quinn's and then saw the look on Ryder's face. She never wanted to see that look again. She knew that he needed to process what he'd seen and heard and she was glad that he seemed to realize that Mark was unimportant to her and that what they had was real and solid.

Ryder was in an unusually good mood Saturday

night as they shared a drink after a very busy and long night. It was their best night of the year so far and Bethany was still feeling the warm fuzzies from the review on Quinn's that was published that morning. Marcia had brought it into the restaurant and plunked it down on the table where they were sitting and drinking their coffee.

"We should frame this and hang it on the wall. We've never had a review like this one before," she said proudly.

Ryder picked up the paper and read the review out loud. It was full of accolades about the food and the service. What made Bethany happiest of all was the final line,

"If you're looking for the kind of comfort food that you wish your mother was able to make, come to Quinn's. You won't be disappointed. This is Manhattan quality fare in Quinn Valley. A true gem."

"A true gem," Ryder repeated holding her gaze until she felt herself beginning to blush and looked away.

"That's really great news," she'd said.

The mood all day had felt celebratory and when Ryder walked her to her car at the end of the night, the kiss they shared made her toes tingle.

"I'll be by late tomorrow afternoon, around three," he said.

~

AT THREE O'CLOCK SHARP, THERE WAS A KNOCK AT the front door. Bethany heard it open and her mother's voice mixed with Ryder's. She took one last look in the mirror before heading downstairs. It was chilly out and since they were going outside to see his lake property, she'd dressed for warmth in a thick fisherman's knit sweater, turtle neck, jeans, heavy socks and her favorite old brown boots that were soft and warm.

When she came downstairs, Ryder and her mother were speaking softly. Her mother looked up and stopped talking. There was a gleam in her eye that Bethany hadn't seen in a long time. Her spirits had been great ever since she got the good news from her doctor.

"Have fun you two," she called out as they stepped outside.

"Do you have a hat?" Ryder asked before they got to his car.

"I do. I forgot to put it on." Bethany fished a knit hat out of her tote bag and pulled it on. She knew it wasn't the most flattering look, but it kept her warm. Ryder was wearing a thick knit hat as well and a down jacket. She had a thin down jacket over her sweater and even though it was cold out, she was warm enough.

"I made us a thermos of hot chocolate we can have when we get to the lake," Ryder said.

They reached his street fifteen minutes later, and he slowed as he reached a large empty lot that overlooked a large lake. There were boat ramps along the shore and the view from his land was beautiful.

"Come on, I'll give you the grand tour." He grabbed the thermos and a blanket and led the way around his lot and down to the shore. There was plenty of room for him to add a dock if he wanted to and he would have a large sunny view almost anywhere on the lot that he decided to build.

"What do you think?"

"It's awesome. I can see why you want to keep it for yourself."

He spread out the blanket and sat Indian-style with the thermos in front of him. He had two plastic mugs with him as well and poured out some hot chocolate for both of them. Bethany joined him on the blanket and gratefully accepted a mug of the steaming beverage. It smelled wonderful and had tiny marshmallows bobbing over the top.

They talked again about the kind of house he wanted to build and she told him all about what she envisioned her dream kitchen looking like. It was fun to dream even if it was for someone else's house.

"So, could you ever see yourself living here?" he surprised her by asking. His tone was serious, and she turned and the love that was reflected in his eyes took her breath away. She nodded. "Yes, of course."

He smiled, then stood up, which confused her, until he bent down on one knee and fished something out of his pocketed. A small, black velvet box. She hadn't expected this at all, not today.

His smile was shaky but about as big as she'd ever seen it.

"Bethany, there's no one else I want to be with. No one else I'd rather live in my dream house with. Our dream house. I want to build it the way we want it. I don't think I ever stopped loving you. You're my best friend and the person I want to spend every day with for the rest of my life. Will you marry me?" He held the ring up, and the diamond sparkled in the sunlight.

"Yes, yes of course I'll marry you! I love you too, Ryder. So much."

He stood and pulled her in for a kiss that went on and on. They sat down again and had more hot chocolate and she stared at the ring. It was beautiful, a cushion cut diamond surrounded by a ring of delicate, smaller diamonds in a platinum setting.

"How long have you had this ring?" She wondered when he'd gone shopping for it.

"My mother gave it to me years ago, before you went to Manhattan. She knew I wanted to ask you then. It was her mother's ring."

"And you've had it all this time." Bethany stared at the ring in wonder.

"Well, it's not like I had anyone else I wanted to give it to." He grinned and pulled her in for another kiss.

"Do you mind if I wait until after the house is built? I want to give my mother some time to get used to the idea."

"I don't mind waiting. She already knows though."

"She does?"

"That's what we were talking about before you

came downstairs. I was asking her permission. She thoroughly approves."

"Oh, well we could do it sooner then."

"How about in a few months? I know my mother is going to have certain ideas about what she wants for a wedding and yours probably will too. That will give them both time to plot and plan. And there's plenty of room in my condo for both of us. We can live there until the house is done."

"I love that plan." She smiled and touched her finger lightly to his lips. "And I love you."

"I love you, too." Ryder kissed her again, and she sighed with happiness. Everything finally was exactly as it should be.

EPILOGUE

Ryder, do twins run in your family by any chance?" Bethany's mother asked as she set three perfect green smoothies on the kitchen table. It was Sunday morning, a little after ten and Ryder had stopped by to show them the house plans. Bethany picked one of the glasses up and took a sip. It was perfect.

"Mom, you've mastered smoothies. This is great!"

"Thank you, dear. Ryder?" She looked eager for his answer.

"I'm thinking, sorry. I don't think there are any twins in the family, actually. Why do you ask?"

"Hmmm. Well, I had the strangest dream last night. It was right after I'd drifted off to sleep and I was holding my crystals in my right hand, snuggled close to my chest. When I woke, it was all so vivid, and so real."

"What was it?" Bethany asked. It was the first time she could remember her mother mentioning any of her dreams.

"It was lovely. I felt sad when it ended. I was in a beautiful garden, just relaxing, when three tiny fairies appeared. They were laughing and dancing and they kept saying the word 'twins' and then both of your names. Isn't that just the strangest thing?"

"That is strange. Did they say anything else?" Bethany asked.

"No. They faded away, and I woke up."

Ryder wrapped his arms around Bethany from behind and kissed her cheek. "Twins would be awesome," he said.

Bethany laughed. "We're getting way ahead of ourselves. We need to get married first."

"About that. How does four months from now sound? Bryan Baker, the builder says he can get it done by then. And that should give you time to plan whatever kind of wedding you want." Ryder grinned as he opened the cardboard tube and laid out the building blueprints.

"Finished in four months? That seems so fast," Bethany said.

"Oh, honey it will go by in a flash," her mother agreed. "But it still gives us plenty of time to plan a lovely wedding."

Ryder showed them the plans, and they were all impressed. It was one thing to talk about what you wanted your dream house to look like. It was something different to see it all laid out in black and white. The house looked amazing.

"Want to take a drive out there?" Ryder asked.

They said goodbye to her mother and drove out to the lot. The air was cool, but the sun was shining as they strolled to the shore of the lake. Ryder rolled out the blueprints on a large, flat rock and they went over them again. It was easier to visualize the house as they stood on the lot where it would be. Bethany smiled up at Ryder.

"This doesn't seem real."

He pulled her into his arms and gently touched his lips to hers.

"It is perfect. We're going to live the rest of our lives right here on this spot and who knows, maybe a year from now, we'll be a family of four."

"Twins. My mother's never dreamed anything like that before."

He grinned. "Fairies and twins. It would be pretty amazing. But a baby or two is just a bonus whenever they decide to come. I love you, and I just can't wait to live here with you, and start our lives together."

"Me too," Bethany said softly, and then she kissed him.

Thank you so much for reading! I hope you enjoyed Bethany and Ryder's story. My next book in this series will be Maggie's story, Calling Charlie, which will be out in April. Before then though, I'll be releasing the first book in a new series set on Nantucket, The Nantucket Inn. It's a family saga series, with sister and brothers and mothers and crazy uncles and lots of small town drama. If you'd like an email notification when it releases, please sign up for my email list.

Visit my website, at www.pamelakelley.com to sign up.

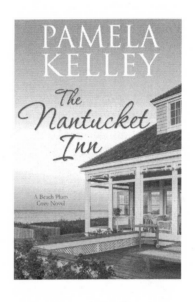